"I must have

Lawrence Carruthers crushed Dora to him and kissed her, tenderly at first, then with a demanding passion.

"Sir!" she whispered, pulling back.

"Please say it. Say you want me, too," he murmured.

Dora wriggled out of his grasp. Who would have thought the offer of a *carte blanche* could be such an unsettling, tempting situation?

"No," she ground out. "How dare you? I'd never have believed you would really ask this of me, Mr. Carruthers. Have you no shame, no delicacy...at all?" She then ran down the path toward the house as fast as she could.

Carruthers's eyebrows knotted together in a scowl. He didn't doubt but that she was no ordinary spinster: melting in his arms one moment, accusing him of indelicacy the next. What he did doubt was that he would ever willingly go near the woman again.

Other books by Margaret Westhaven

MISS DALRYMPLE'S VIRTUE

FALSE IMPRESSIONS

MARGARET WESTHAVEN

Harlequin Books

TORONTO • NEW YORK • LONDON
AMSTERDAM • PARIS • SYDNEY • HAMBURG
STOCKHOLM • ATHENS • TOKYO • MILAN

Published July 1989

ISBN 0-373-31106-0

CHAPTER ONE

"DORA, I CAN'T have heard you properly. I entreat you to be serious!" exclaimed Lady Fitzhugh, casting a worried look round the comfortable drawing room of her country house, as though unseen ears might have been party to the words which had just shocked her. "You always were such a spirited, lighthearted child," she added with a glance of appeal.

Theodora Thornfield placed her fringe-work upon the table and gazed at her sister with calm eyes. "Really, Mary, I'm no longer a child—indeed, I'll soon be nine-and-twenty—and I tell you again, quite seriously, that I intend to do it."

Lady Fitzhugh's pleasant round face crinkled in its customary prelude to a shower of tears. "But why?" she wailed with no semblance of dignity. "You must really be saying that Sir Leonard and the children, or even I, have made you unhappy here, and so you wish to abandon us all!" She dissolved into the expected damp state.

Dora got up to comfort her stricken sister. Mary had a talent for tears; all of Dora's elder sisters were rather managing souls in their different ways, and Mary's particular style of manipulation had always been irksome.

"Dear Mary," said Dora, as she dabbed at her sister's eyes with a handkerchief, "Papa has been dead for over a year now. When he was alive I was quite busy and useful. But ever since his death—" she cast down her eyes at these words, for she hadn't given up grieving for their kindly, if thoughtless, father "—I've done nothing but pay visits to my sisters. Five months in Scotland with Blanche and Lord MacDonald; four months with Lavinia's family in Kent; and now this time with you and Sir Leonard. I haven't had a home of my own, Mary."

"But what has that got to do with turning yourself into a paid companion?" Mary demanded. "Of course Thorne Park was entailed, and even if our awful cousin hadn't inherited it, you couldn't have stayed on there alone. Your home is with Sir Leonard and me now." The last words were meant to be spoken with a comforting sense of finality. "You *are* a silly girl," Mary added for emphasis.

Dora returned to her seat, shaking her head. "Dear, I'm a single woman with scarcely any income. I must *do* something. I want to earn my own way in the world, rather than..." She hesitated. How to explain to this beloved but oversensitive sister that one was simply tired of being what could only be described as a professional aunt? Mary, Blanche and Lavinia were all unfailingly kind to Dora, as were their respective families, but there was the inevitable tendency to leave any disagreeable task as a matter of course to a maiden lady with nothing better to do. It wasn't the tasks one minded so much as the offhanded requests that accompanied them. Upon the unexpected offer of a post, Dora had instantly decided that, if her fate were to fetch and carry, she'd at least be paid formally for the indignity.

"A pity you didn't wed when you had the chance," sighed Mary.

Dora winced. Mary never let a day go by without harping on this particular theme; nor did her other two sisters. It had been a long year.

"That dashing baronet who ran after you during your London season. Or even the clergyman, Mr. Ball. He's now rector of a parish not five miles from here. How convenient that would have been for us all.''

"You seem to forget, sister, that I didn't wish to marry either Sir John or Mr. Ball, and that makes all your regrets futile," put in Dora.

"There were others," Mary insisted with another noisy sigh. Theodora had really been quite a beauty as a young girl, and in spite of her lack of dowry she had had plenty of admirers. Her looks hadn't diminished with the years, though naturally enough the number of her suitors had. With those cool but haunting grey eyes, that flaxen hair and her lovely figure, Dora was the image of poor Mama, and quite the beauty of the family. Why on earth hadn't the tiresome girl turned all these assets to account, rather than wasting her most marriageable years playing piquet with dear Papa?

While Mary's thoughts roved in this direction, Dora was also thinking of her lost youth. Her orderly mind skimmed briefly over the memory of each unsuccessful suitor; for, since she had never been in love, she didn't regret her rejection of any of them. She concentrated rather on the innocent good times she'd enjoyed in Sussex, where she'd been mistress of Thorne Park and, because the Park was the noblest residence in the neighbourhood and the Thornfields the oldest family, the acknowledged leader of local society. Strange that she should have been so heedless of the future, for it hadn't been reasonable to expect to go on forever in such a pleasant way. Her father's death had put an effective end to Dora's dreamlike existence, and the subsequent disclosure of his bleak financial state had left her practically penniless, under the protection of her three brothers-in-law. From mistress of an estate to meek maiden aunt had been a sudden change for one so proud as Dora, but she flattered herself that she'd learned humility in the year since

Papa's death. There was no use in sighing over a youth that had passed. The once carefree and pretty Miss Thornfield was getting on. She was already wearing caps, despite her sisters' protests that she was much too young.

"Lady Bracken's letter was most kind, and she *is* our cousin, you know," Dora said coaxingly, for she didn't intend to drop the subject. "I won't be going out to strangers. And remember that it was she who chaperoned me during my first season in London."

"Your *only* season," Mary added bitterly. "And I've often thought that she might have given you another, as she's our only relation who spends any length of time in town."

Dora forbore to mention that if she herself had been Lady Bracken, she would have seen no reason to give more than a few months' time to a distant young cousin. "My dear, that was over ten years ago. Would you have me still under Lady Bracken's wing at my age? There is a limit." She couldn't help laughing at the thought of a lady of her mature years still being carefully brought out each year, dusted off and displayed in the marriage market. Such things did happen, but they weren't to Dora's taste.

"And who are these Brackens anyway? Cousin Maud is a dreadful person. Aside from your one season, she's never paid the least heed to our branch of the family. She didn't write to us at the time of Papa's death, when it would have been proper, and the only gesture she makes now is to offer to turn my sister into a servant! The gall of that woman..." And Mary, shaking her head and brushing away a few more tears, gave way to incoherent mutterings of disparagement.

"I remember our cousin as a better hostess than she was a correspondent," Dora said laughing. "Fashionable and thoughtless. I know her better than you, since I stayed with her. I wasn't shocked when she didn't write at the time of the funeral. But I was surprised, and pleased, to get her letter the other day. Perhaps you don't realize, Mary, that Cousin Maud is bringing her daughter out this season. One thing she needs me for, she says, is to help chaperone little Augusta. You know how I love London! She wishes me to join the family there within the month."

"A chaperone! You!" Mary glared at a perfectly innocent fireplace screen which Dora had worked for her just last winter; it was obvious that the screen was, for the moment, taking the place of Cousin Maud.

"Chaperones aren't servants, Mary," Dora put in cagily.

"They're little more when they also serve as paid companions! What of this chit, Maud's daughter? Are you to go about in the wake of some selfish young beauty who'll browbeat you and rob you of all your dignity?"

Sighing and biting back a few choice, cutting words about the similar lack of dignity she had been labouring under as a poor relation in her sisters' houses, Dora answered, "This is a godsend, Mary, not a tragedy. Make up your mind to it. I'm going to live with the Brackens, and that's that. I posted my letter to Cousin Maud this very morning."

Mary gasped. It had never occurred to her that Theodora had been presenting her with a fait accompli. It was inconceivable that her sister should actually have taken steps for the future without consulting Mary or, more importantly, Sir Leonard. The dressing-bell sounded before Mary could think of an adequately quelling reply to Dora's revelation, and she decided to broach the matter with her husband before dinner and let *him* deal with his headstrong sister-in-law.

While Dora performed her simple evening toilette, she was mistakenly at peace about her future. It was a bit odd that Mary had made no answer to the news that her sister had gone ahead and accepted the wretched post, but at least there hadn't been another unpleasant scene. Dora would have been quite surprised had she witnessed the small drama being enacted that very moment in Lady Fitzhugh's dressing room.

Sir Leonard Fitzhugh, his eyes bulging with disbelief, was responding in character to his wife's information. "Damme!" he cried, pulling up his rather stocky figure to its full height. "I won't have Theodora running about the countryside, giving the world every reason to think we've driven her from our home!"

"My dear, I'm sure you can explain to Dora why we mustn't allow her to do any such thing," replied Mary confidently. In situations where she herself was inclined to dissolve into a watering pot, Sir Leonard could always be relied upon to argue both sternly and loudly, and such an approach was bound to be effective with Dora. "But do, please, my dear, take care to watch your temper before my sister," she added. "Dora has never been shouted at."

"Then high time she was," muttered Sir Leonard, and the pair made ready to descend.

BEFORE THE EVENING WAS OVER Sir Leonard had indeed shouted, Dora had responded with icy calmness, and Mary had burst into tears. This last occurred just before tea was brought into the drawing room, where the three were sitting in a not very harmonious state. Patting her sister's hand while her brother-in-law hovered solicitously behind his wife—for Lady Fitzhugh's dramatics had never yet failed to bring her husband round to comparative mildness—Dora searched her mind for some way of bringing the debate to an end, to the satisfaction of all parties.

"My dear brother," she finally said in her sweetest voice, with an entreating look into Sir Leonard's glowering face, "as I see it, the only reason you object to my going to Lady

Bracken is the fear that the world will think you've treated me badly. Isn't that so?''

Sir Leonard started. ''No, not at all. We'd miss your company, too, Theodora,'' he said with a glance at his wife. Then he strode back to his chair on the other side of the fire, as though a return to the evening's argument would best be taken up from his own territory.

''I flatter myself that I've contrived to be useful,'' responded Dora at her most demure. She knew that her brother-in-law was fond enough of her, but any husband must be alarmed at the prospect of his wife's sister settling into his home for life. She was shrewdly counting on Sir Leonard's normalcy in this respect.

''Useful! Oh, Dora,'' wailed Mary, and it was only after many soft words of affection on Dora's part that her ladyship was calm again.

When her sister's sniffles had quietened, Dora tried again. ''I believe that all I have to do is make it known to my acquaintance that I'm not leaving your protection because I'm estranged from you. I still correspond with Amelia Lavenham in London, my friend from school, and I can trust her to spread the word. As for Blanche and Lavinia, they can't blame you for allowing me to take up the post. I'll merely tell them, as I've told you, that I wish to make my own way in life.'' She paused. She was far past one-and-twenty, and her own mistress; she really didn't need to cajole and plead with her family before doing anything she thought fit. But she did understand that they expected it.

Sir Leonard gave a bark halfway between a laugh and a shout of disapproval. ''As for your town friends, I've no interest in the opinion of the ton,'' he said in the careless way of the confirmed country gentleman. ''But,'' he added, ''I must warn you, Theodora, that your fine dreams of independence will come to nothing. Companion, indeed!''

Dora sighed. "I know it won't be pleasant," she admitted. "It won't be anything like independence. In fact..." Her words drifted away. She'd been about to say that she could think of few things worse, but such a statement would betray how intolerable she found her present life. Yet finish her sentence she must, for both Mary and Sir Leonard were looking at her expectantly. "If my income were larger," she said lamely, "I'd love to set myself up in a cottage of my own." It was with reluctance that she thus exposed one of her pet fancies to Sir Leonard's probable derision.

Mary took up this news with joy. "But surely that can be, Dora," she cried. "Sir Leonard will make you a present of a small cottage in the neighbourhood, and we'll look out for a companion for *you*."

Out of the corner of her eye Dora saw Sir Leonard wince at his wife's expensive suggestion. That was a relief! She didn't want the Fitzhughs to place her under such a heavy obligation, no matter how kindly meant. She declined Mary's offer, adding that she hoped a mere companion would be welcome as a visitor in the future, whenever Lady Bracken might grant a short holiday.

In assuring their sister that she'd always be welcome under their roof, Sir Leonard and his lady quite lost sight of the fact that Theodora had carried her point, and that her future position was indeed a settled thing.

NEXT MORNING at the breakfast table it was Mary who made the first allusion to the delicate subject. "We'll look over your clothes at once," she said placidly enough, nodding at Dora. "If you are really going to London, you'll need a complete fitting out."

Dora laughed as she looked up from her coffee. "I don't believe that a paid companion is expected to shine socially," she offered for her sister's edification.

"You shall," said Mary. "If you're to chaperone the Bracken child, you'll go to parties—"

"Where I'll sit against the wall and watch my charge," broke in Dora, still in a cheerful-enough voice, though indeed the thought of chaperoning a young lady, rather than being one, was already beginning to depress her.

Mary sniffed. "No, you won't. And even if you should, there's no reason to sit at a ton party looking like a dowd. Besides, men will see you and fall in love with you, for how could they help it? And then you'll be sorry not to have a new dress."

"My dear Mary, you needn't think that I intend to use this association with the Brackens to push myself in where spinsters are seldom wanted or needed," Dora said in a harsh voice which made both her sister and her brother-in-law jump, so out of character was it. Then, recovering herself, she added with a laugh, "I'll be what I'm hired to be: Lady Bracken's humble companion, properly grateful for whatever crumbs are thrown my way."

"If you'll take my advice, Theodora, you won't run on to the Brackens about crumbs and such," said Sir Leonard. He rattled his newspaper for emphasis.

"Oh, dear, no." Dora made haste to agree, looking at her brother-in-law in amazement. She'd never thought Sir Leonard was the type to appreciate a satirical remark.

Meanwhile, Mary was giggling at the thought of crumbs being thrown her regal-looking sister. "You must come right back to us if the post is too much for you, dear," she directed. "This is your home."

"Kind Mary! I know, and I'll miss you, Sir Leonard, and the children terribly." Dora skimmed over the truth a bit, for the four boys were little terrors, though she did love them. She felt she would love them even more at a distance.

"Poor dear!" Mary hovered delicately at the edge of tears for a moment, then collected herself. "Well! I do mean to see that your clothes are fit for any occasion, for one never knows what might happen. No argument! It will be my parting gift to you." She looked to her husband for approval and was granted a curt nod. A dress or two wouldn't put a man out of pocket, one could almost see Sir Leonard thinking, and he was lucky to have escaped the cottage suggestion.

Dora didn't protest too much at the offer of clothing. She was grateful for her sister's generosity, as her tiny income from Mama's estate didn't allow her to do much more than replace her stockings. But at the same time it seemed a shame that Mary's fine taste must be wasted on the quiet and modest things which Dora, in the grip of impending middle age, felt compelled to wear now she was out of mourning.

She couldn't know that Mary, keeping her own counsel, was deviously planning to fit her sister out in the finest and most unspinsterly garb possible. Dora's new ideas on dress were absurd and could be worked around. The more she thought about it, the more Lady Fitzhugh was inclined to look on her sister's move as another chance at matrimony. It had always been Mary's belief—and she knew sisters Blanche and Lavinia shared it—that the youngest Miss Thornfield couldn't be so beautiful for nothing!

CHAPTER TWO

"MARY, THE DRESSMAKER'S made a terrible mistake with the blue silk," said Dora, rustling into her sister's dressing room a couple of weeks later. "It was kind of you to wish me to have a ball gown, and I shan't scold you for ordering it behind my back, but I look like a Cyprian!"

Mary glanced up from the letter she was reading and broke into a smile. "Dora, you're lovely! And say what you will, I refuse to make you up a brown stuff ball gown with a black bow at the neck, or whatever other absurd getup you think proper for a spinster."

Dora had to laugh, but she remained determined. "Say what *you* will, sister, I won't trick myself out like a dashing female when I'm nothing of the sort. I know just what to do, though, and I've already told the seamstress. We're to fill the neckline in with that lace I took off my old white gown, and match a bit of blue satin ribbon to go round the throat. That will make this modest enough for a female in my situation."

Mary shuddered. "Dora, however do you expect to catch a husband in a revolting costume like that? Leave the gown as it is."

"I am not trying to catch a husband, I'll have you know," stated Dora. Perhaps she did still cherish dreams of finding the right man, but she knew them to be ridiculous and never admitted them to a soul. Shaking her head, she surveyed herself in Mary's pier glass. The gown, with its stylish and sophisticated cut, was wildly at odds with the grey-ribboned cap that sat atop her curls. But the cap reminded Dora of exactly where her fate, if not her interest, lay.

Mary was retorting, "Why, any number of men will rush to attach you once you're back on the market."

"On the market! Please."

"And," Mary continued, "I've just been reading a letter from sister Lavinia, and I beg you, Dora, even if you don't wish to marry, do not, whatever you do, write to Lavinia of your feelings. She's delighted that you're to make an appearance in town. But she doesn't mince words about the companion business, either." She held the paper slightly farther away from her and read, "'Tell Dora she is being unspeakably foolish, and she'd do better to come back to me in Kent. Maud Bracken will take full advantage of keeping one of our family as a domestic. However, the chance to get to town again should really not be missed, and I cannot offer that.' And then she goes on to say that you're sure to take."

"My letter from Blanche sounded just like that," Dora admitted, poking at the revealing neckline of her new dress. No matter what she did, she couldn't make any more of her person disappear within the silken bodice. "Perhaps a simple lace trimming round the neck edge?" she suggested.

Mary snorted. "Ruin that gown at your peril, my dear. You'll need to make a good appearance in town if Amelia Lavenham is to stand your friend, as I'm sure she will. Such a dear, sweet young woman, and I've heard she gives such lovely parties. Ah, sometimes I quite envy you, Dora. Sir Leonard won't go near London."

"No more will any of my brothers-in-law," answered Dora. "In point of fact, Mary, that was my biggest reason for accepting this post."

She was reminded of another when, three seconds later, Mary casually asked her to look in on the schoolroom after she'd changed out of the new gown. When Mary said look in on the schoolroom, she meant entertain her four little angels for the rest of the day so that the nursemaid and governess might lend a hand with the housework.

Dora cheerfully complied with her sister's wishes, but she took comfort in the fact that, in the very near future, she would be earning a salary for doing easier work than she was now engaged upon. The Brackens had only the one daughter, now grown up. And whatever a companion's duties were, Dora would be performing them in London!

A FEW DAYS LATER, in a certain town house in Albemarle Street, Mr. Lawrence Carruthers ended his morning visit with his friend Sir Giles Bracken and left the baronet in the library. The butler stood ready in the front hall with the gentleman's hat and cane, but there were also two young and giggling chambermaids peering at the handsome visitor from behind a door. Mr. Carruthers did not notice this; the butler did, however, and his black frown soon sent the two youthful miscreants about their business.

Carruthers went out just as a pretty blonde woman, followed by a maid, was raising a gloved hand to the knocker. In his haste he nearly ran the lady down. "Ma'am, I beg your pardon, how thoughtless of me to burst out the door like a cannonball." He gave a warm and winning smile and swept his best bow before looking directly at her. When he did, he started in surprise. Did he know her? Surely not. He would have remembered....

Dora felt her cheeks grow warm. How funny this was! She wished Mary could be here. Or perhaps not. Gentlemen, insisted Mary, would be thronging London this season for the purpose of marrying penniless companions. And here was the first candidate, the fond sister would have exulted.

This man was better looking and more distinguished than anyone Dora could have thought up, though probably Mary would have been able to imagine him very well. He straightened from his bow to smile down at Dora from a very great height indeed; for she was a tall woman, and her nose was only at a level with his snowy cravat. A pair of remarkably broad shoulders were encased in a coat sleeker and more finely cut than any Dora had seen since her long-ago first season; and the gentleman's classic features were set off by dark hair in a Brutus crop. His hazel eyes were piercing, and surely that was admiration in them.

"You are forgiven, sir," Dora answered with a distant nod. She felt a twinge of annoyance that this handsome stranger should assess her so boldly; then she blushed as the thought struck her that she was quite as guilty of staring at him. She was hardly in the position to give him a set-down.

The gentleman smiled more widely. "Good day, then, ma'am." And he ran down the steps and headed for a smart curricle, which Dora now noticed for the first time in front of Sir Leonard's heavy old travelling coach.

Dora took a last look at the gentleman and found him observing her, now from the seat of his vehicle. There was something so disturbing about his questioning gaze. They exchanged a last nod, and his smile changed, for an instant, to a caressing expression that made Dora draw in her breath. She must have grown countrified in the years since her last visit to London; the man was probably a flirt who was only treating her with the particularity he offered any chance-met woman.

As he tooled the curricle down Albemarle Street, Carruthers was making up his mind to watch for the blonde woman in the coming days. He began to wish he'd cast aside propriety and introduced himself. Well, no matter; the Brackens were certain to know who the lady was.

Carruthers frowned, wondering if, when run to ground, the blonde would prove to be only another simpering and shallow lady of quality. He might well be indulging in a romantic fancy that she was somehow different, an opinion formed on only one look into her intelligent grey eyes. But in any case Carruthers would find her. It might mean haunting those ton gatherings which bored him; but she was obviously a lady come to town for the season, and he must look for her in the settings ladies preferred. He shrugged at this grim necessity, then he smiled. It had been years since society parties had held any attraction for Lawrence Carruthers; he knew his presence at the season's routs and balls would engender some amusing speculation. The gossips would say he was hanging out for a wife.

Dora was forcing herself to take her mind off handsome men and look up at the house. The narrow, dignified residence was quite as she remembered it, though it was many years since she had last stood before its doors, a shy young lady who had never been out of Sussex, except to go to school. How daunting it had been to meet her relations, the Brackens, for the first time, Dora thought, with an indulgent smile for the green young thing she had been. She looked up at the windows, trying to remember which had been her own room. It had been a large chamber, looking down on the busy street, which had delighted the country-bred and curious Dora. But how she had wished that one of her sisters could have presented her, rather than a distant cousin! It would have been so much more comfortable. But Mary had been on the point of lying-in with her first; Blanche in faraway Scotland had also been at some inconvenient stage of the breeding process; and Lavinia had been staying at her husband's plantation in the West Indies. The Brackens had been Dora's only chance.

And so were they now, she mused with a little sigh.

"Madam?" The butler, a stately, elderly man, was addressing her.

Dora came out of her dreamy state and nodded briskly. "I'm certain you don't remember me, Greaves, after ten or more years, but I'm Miss Thornfield. I—" a second's pause paid homage to the first time she had ever stated her new position in life "—I've come to be Lady Bracken's companion. They expect me."

"To be sure, Miss Thornfield." And with respectful manners that quite set Dora's mind at rest as to the treatment a companion would receive from this staff, Greaves took over the disposition of her party. Mary's abigail was sent to refresh herself before the drive home; Dora's baggage disappeared up the stairs; and Dora herself was led into the morning room at the back of the house, there to wait until Greaves could announce her to Sir Giles and her ladyship, who were both at home.

Dora resisted a strong impulse to question the butler on the identity of the gentleman she had just encountered. He must have been a guest of Sir Giles's; the two men might be of an age, considered Dora, remembering that Sir Giles Bracken would be forty now. She had observed the light touch of grey at the stranger's temples. The effect had been most attractive, only adding to the gentleman's distinguished appearance.

Left alone, Dora put the stranger from her mind and wandered about the morning room, trying to concentrate on the furnishings. She couldn't really remember what this chamber had looked like years ago, but it certainly had the air of recent redecoration. A profusion of floral chintzes and embroidered velvet draperies brought back with a rush memories of Cousin Maud's taste. Dora used to admire all her cousin's things unreservedly. Formal, but without fault, was her more considered judgement now as she let her hand rest on the back of a pretty Queen Anne chair.

She was about to settle herself near the crackling wood fire when an odd, choking sound made her turn about. The noise seemed to be coming from the window seat, and she headed there. It was odd that the draperies were pulled shut at this time of the morning. The sound grew louder the closer Dora got to the window. Yes, it was definitely someone crying!

Gently she drew back the velvet drapery. A young girl was curled into the window seat; her pale, pointed face half-hidden in a lacy handkerchief. She gave a little shriek and stared at Dora with frightened blue eyes.

"Augusta?" Dora asked with a reassuring smile, certain that the child must be the daughter of the house. She had grown up to be elegant, if not very pretty. The sprigged muslin gown was expensive, and the mouse-brown hair fashionably cut and curled. "It's Cousin Theodora, my dear. When I last saw you you were a child of six!"

"Cousin Theodora!" The girl jumped up and made a curtsey, wringing the handkerchief in her hands as she bobbed up and down. "I'm very sorry. I never meant to make such a dis—display of myself, but you see, I thought I was alone— Oh!" Her face disappeared into the white cloth again as the tears overtook her.

"Would you care to tell me what's troubling you, dear?" Dora ventured, putting one arm around the child and leading her to a sofa. They both sat down, Augusta rubbing at her eyes and reddened nose in a valiant effort to calm herself.

She ended this process by blowing her nose loudly, then gave Dora a solicitous glance. "I—I really shouldn't tell you."

"Then don't. Forgive me for asking," was Dora's prompt reply. She was a very private person herself, and besides, it was early days to be meddling in the affairs of anyone in her new home.

"But," Augusta continued quickly, "I would very much like you to know, if we are to be friends. And we are, aren't we?"

"Of course!" Charmed by such artless goodwill, Dora was quite ready to be Augusta's confidante. Unless... "It isn't a quarrel with your mama, is it?" she asked, certain that it would do her own position no good if she were to be listening to tales of ill-use from her new employer's daughter.

"No, Mama and I never quarrel. It's simply that she— and Papa—are being quite unreasonable," Augusta stated, her red-rimmed eyes scanning her cousin's face. She seemed to relax a little as she read the sympathy in the pretty features of her relation.

Dora was indeed feeling sorry for the child by now, for she had made a guess at the problem; and not a wild guess, either, considering Augusta's age and the very real distress she was labouring under. "Could this have to do with a young man?"

Augusta stared. "Why, how did you know, Cousin Theodora? It's simply horrid that Mama and Papa can't understand how I feel, for they must have been young once, and possibly even in love. I'm in absolute misery, Cousin, and the thought of remaining in London for months and months without a sight of my Edgar has me ready to—to throw things, and climb up the walls, and run away back to Surrey."

"Your Edgar?" prompted Dora. A very definite feeling of relief swept over her, for it had crossed her mind that her young cousin might possibly be crying over the handsome gentleman whom Dora had seen on the steps of the house. But the Edgar in question was obviously not in London.

It took no more than these two words to make the whole story come pouring forth. Augusta had been suffering for someone to confide in for, not yet officially out and on her first visit to London, she hadn't yet made friends of her own age. Dora learned in the next five minutes that the mysterious Edgar's surname was Farley, and that he was a young clergyman who lived in Augusta's neighbourhood in the country. He had only recently been ordained, Augusta explained with a proprietary air, and hadn't yet obtained a curacy or a living. Not only that, but he, his widowed mother and spinster sister had to make do on a very small income indeed. The Farleys were positively scraping to get by. For these reasons Augusta's parents hadn't smiled upon Edgar's attachment to Augusta, though, as the young girl put it, they had loved each other "for years."

"And I can't feature why they insist that I marry a man with money," she exclaimed in frustration. "How can my own papa and mama be so mercenary when they know my happiness is at stake? Besides, I have a fortune of my own, or so they tell me, and Edgar and I might be quite comfortable living on that. You don't think it matters which one has the money, do you, Cousin Theodora? As long as there is enough?"

"Why, I've never given such matters much thought," Dora admitted. "But look at your parents' side of things. Your mama has been longing to present you to London society since you were born, I should wager. Think, you're their only child, and your presentation must mean the world to them. Why not simply make up your mind to enjoy the season—and you will, Augusta, I'm certain of it—and remain constant to your clergyman? Your mother and father might relent if they see that the young man is the only one who'll make you happy." Dora kept to herself what she really thought: that no case of calf-love was likely to survive the whirl of London, especially if the girl in question found other admirers. And a young, rather sweet-looking debutante with a goodly portion would have no shortage of those.

Augusta gave a deep sigh. "We've sworn to remain true no matter what," she said in quiet, dramatic tones. "You've got our plan exactly, Cousin. But—" her voice trembled "—I simply hadn't realized how very lonely I'd be without him. We used to meet in secret nearly every day, you know, in the churchyard. Oh, I simply can't bear the thought of months of this!"

"How long have you been in town?" Dora enquired.

"Nearly a week," the girl replied bleakly with a twist of the damp scrap of lace-trimmed linen. There was an ominous sound of tearing fabric.

Fighting back the urge to laugh at Augusta's youthful dramatics, Dora dug into her reticule and offered a fresh handkerchief, which Augusta tamely sniffed into. Dora was wracking her brain, much as she had just searched her reticule, for more words of comfort, when the door opened and an elegant lady came into the room.

"Cousin Theodora! How delightful to see you at last! Your letter did indicate that you'd be arriving earlier in the day, but I'm quite prepared to forgive you in this instance. I see you and my Augusta have been getting acquainted. Do stand up and let me see you properly, my dear. Ah, yes, you always were rather tall, were you not? Though I did think that Lady Jermyn used to call you a Maypole out of jealousy pure and simple, for she was after Sir John Webberley, you know, and he was mad for you. Ah! How very many years have gone by. I was so sorry to hear about your father, Cousin, and I said to Sir Giles, ask him if I did not, 'Why don't we have poor Theodora Thornfield to be my companion? She'll be alone in the world now, but for her three sisters, and I've been wanting a companion this age.' And Sir Giles said..."

This torrent of words dazzled Dora as she obediently stood up to face Cousin Maud, Lady Bracken, whom she had not seen since she herself was eighteen. Her ladyship was a dark, handsome woman whose aristocratic profile was being refined by the passage of years into something more hawklike than Dora remembered. It came back to her only now that the lady was a very great talker indeed. Dora also seemed to recall that, as the conversation of Cousin Maud allowed for no pauses, she wasn't offended by interruptions.

"How do you do, Cousin Maud?" Dora therefore interjected into the middle of Lady Bracken's account of what Sir Giles had said.

"Cousin!" Lady Bracken was quite ready to do her possible to make the new arrival welcome. She clasped Dora's gloved hands, and the two ladies' cheeks brushed. "Now I'm sure you'll be wanting to see your room and take off your outdoor things. What a very interesting pelisse, my dear. Is it new? Why had I supposed you would still be in mourning."

"Papa has been gone more than a year," Dora explained, wondering what the word "interesting" was meant to convey. She thought that her new fawn merino pelisse, and the plumed bonnet she wore with it, were the prettiest things she had worn in years. Mary had chosen both, and Dora's only fear had been that these, like the new ball gown, might be considered too dashing—or too young—for a paid companion. Perhaps that was what Cousin Maud had meant. Well, one could hardly ask her, so Dora supposed that the best thing to do would be to ignore the remark. Memories were flooding back to her with every moment spent in Lady Bracken's company. Many of Cousin Maud's remarks had had to be ignored, from the well-meaning nonsense to the cattish jibes. And now, ignoring them would be not only good manners, but good business.

The door, which had been left ajar, burst all the way open yet again, and Sir Giles Bracken was the next to come into the morning room. Dora smiled. He had changed but little. His shrewd blue eyes were the same, his lank brown hair only a little grey, and his tall, thin figure still resembled, ever so slightly, that of a stork. "Well, here's our newest addition to the horde of females surrounding me," Sir Giles quipped, taking Dora's hand in both of his. "Welcome, Cousin Theodora. So you've come to help us launch Augusta, have you?"

"Well, not altogether, Sir Giles. She's here to companion *me*," his wife added, to qualify this statement.

"Yes, my dear. I give you fair warning, Cousin," he said as his eyes twinkled mischievously at Dora. "You'll have your hands full with these two."

She gave the most diplomatic answer she could think of: silence and a slight curve of her lips. Then Lady Bracken decided to accompany Dora to her bed chamber. Augusta, who was already looking worshipfully at Theodora in the wake of their intimate talk, fell into step behind them. "For I've put you in a nice, quiet chamber that looks out on the back, knowing that, now you are older, you wouldn't enjoy the noise of the street in one of the big guest rooms," Lady Bracken said, leading the way into the hall, "and I'm sure you'll be very comfortable. I hope you won't be too tired to come out with Augusta and me later on. We're going for a fitting at the modiste's, and there are several little commissions you might do for me while you wait for us, if you'd be so good. I do so hate the crowds one encounters in the shops.''

Dora was guilty of flashing a rather desperate glance at Sir Giles as that gentleman went on his way down the stairs, in the opposite direction of the female procession. He winked at her. She shrugged, wishing she might stay with the baronet, to ask him, among other things, who the friend was who had been visiting him not half an hour before.

"Oh, Cousin Theodora, I'm so glad you're here," said Augusta, trotting along by Dora's side as they mounted the stairs behind Lady Bracken.

Dora smiled her answer. Taking the good with the bad, she had to agree with the child. She was glad to be in Albemarle Street, even when a few moments later it proved that Cousin Maud had stuck her new companion into a very modest chamber at the back of the house, a room that bore no comparison to the one Dora had used years ago, as a guest.

CHAPTER THREE

SOME WEEKS LATER, Dora had cause to be displeased with her new lot in life. Outwardly, she was in the best of circumstances. Dressed in the most fashionable gown she'd owned in years—the blue silk which had caused her and Mary to have words, and which she had finally agreed not to "ruin"—she was attending Lady Vining's ball, one of the acknowledged annual highlights of the London season. The Vinings' grand ballroom glittered and shimmered under a blaze of crystal chandeliers, and it was thronged with more fashionable people than Dora had seen in the years since she had last been in the metropolis. But—lowering thought!—instead of taking part in the cotillion in progress, as she would have done a decade ago, Dora was seated on a small gilt chair on the sidelines, firmly established in the role of chaperone to Miss Augusta Bracken. And not a successful chaperone, either, for Augusta was fidgeting and tapping her feet from a chair at Dora's side.

"Oh, Cousin!" whispered the girl. "I'll simply die of shame! What if I sit out every dance?"

"Now, dear, you know we arrived just as this dance was starting. A young man would have had to be very quick to ask you. Besides, I understood that you weren't on the lookout for admirers," Dora answered with a little smile. She was becoming very attached to this child, who, once she had got over the melancholy first days of homesickness and separation from her longtime beau, had begun to show every sign of enjoying her season.

"Well, of course you're in on my secret, Dora," Augusta murmured, "but even though I don't want to marry anyone but dear Edgar, now that I am in London, and out, I certainly want to dance! And so should you, Cousin. I'm so very glad you could come with us tonight!"

"Your mama had the headache, and you needed a chaperone," Dora answered serenely. As it happened, this was Dora's first social evening since she had arrived, for Lady Bracken hadn't had the headache for Augusta's court presentation, nor for the young girl's all-important first appearance at Almack's. And Dora had modestly declined to go with the Brackens unless she was needed in her official capacity. "Chaperones, my dear, do not dance," she added.

"Nonsense! Mama's been known to."

"But she is the lady of a baronet, not a paid companion."

Augusta glared. "Cousin Dora, you drive me wild with these meek airs. I warn you, before the season is out I'll have found a gentleman to marry you. Why shouldn't I, in the time I save from not having to look out for one for myself?"

Dora let a peal of laughter escape her and patted her young charge on the arm. "My dear, you're incorrigible! Please don't put it about that I'm looking for a husband. Absurd, at my age."

Augusta snorted, a most unladylike sound coming from so small and delicate a creature. "If you are somewhat older than I, you're still lovely as a picture. Oh, never you fear, Cousin. I'll match you with someone."

"My sisters have been saying the same thing for years," Dora responded airily. "I give you leave to try the impossible. Now! Isn't that Ensign Fox heading this way, looking very red of ear?''

Augusta sat up straighter and adjusted the folds of her white gauze gown.

The very young military man had soon bowed before the ladies, and with much shuffling of feet and a few discreet coughs, he solicited the honour of the next dance with Miss Bracken.

Dora waved them away with a light heart, glad that her duties were taking care of themselves. It was very curious, but she felt the same anxiety that Augusta must dance every dance which she used to feel, many years ago, on her own account.

And now, with Augusta safely out on the floor, Dora realized that her chagrin of a few moments before had completely flown out of her mind. It made no difference that she wouldn't be dancing. It was a wonderful treat merely to observe the others. How she did love London! And how very much she had missed these brightly clothed crowds. Dora settled herself in to enjoy the spectacle vicariously, like any lady of uncertain age.

As she sat smiling at the dancers, Sir Giles wound his way back to her chair. ''Well, Cousin,'' he said jovially, ''I've made my little social circle about the room. And I've already presented you to Lady Vining, should you be wanting her for anything, and if you are quite comfortable...''

Dora laughed. Sir Giles was really a dear. She perfectly recognized the manner of a man uninterested in dancing and anxious to be off to the card room, and was about to interrupt her cousin to give him leave to go when she noticed that he had abruptly changed the subject.

''Why, there's Lawrence Carruthers,'' Sir Giles was murmuring. ''A very good friend of mine from Oxford days. First time I've seen him at one of these squeezes. That very tall man, Cousin—over there."

Dora turned in the direction which Sir Giles had indicated. "How interesting. An old friend of yours?" she was saying politely, when she caught sight of the man the baronet was indicating.

And she stared, for standing there, separated from her by two or three groups of people, was the wonderfully handsome man who had nearly bumped into her on the steps of the Bracken house the day of her arrival in town. In the ensuing weeks she had despaired of ever glimpsing him again. But here he was, and surrounded by three stylish, beautiful women. The trio was chattering away, each lady vying for the gentleman's attention, but now and then he allowed his eyes to wander. Suddenly they met Dora's.

She looked away, confused. How horrid to be detected, at her age, in the act of blatantly staring at a man!

"He's coming over," Sir Giles bent down to say. "Must have seen me. Carruthers!" he suddenly cried out, advancing to meet the other man.

"Bracken! I never expected to see you here, you old stick."

"It's a matter of bringing my daughter out," Sir Giles explained. "You know I prefer to live quietly, even when in town."

"Your daughter," remarked Mr. Carruthers thoughtfully. He turned to Dora. "May I have the pleasure of an introduction to the young lady?" His hazel eyes were somewhat puzzled, for there was certainly no resemblance between Dora and Sir Giles Bracken.

"This isn't my daughter, man," Sir Giles said with his barking laugh. "Wife's cousin, Miss Thornfield. May I present Mr. Carruthers?"

Miss Thornfield inclined her head. Mr. Carruthers bent over her hand, holding it for a long moment.

"So here you are at last, madam," said Carruthers. "I'd despaired of finding you again. Last week at the theatre I even asked your cousin, Lady Bracken, to identify you to me, but she said she didn't know anyone of your description."

"Did you? Did she?" responded Dora, very confused. He had been looking for her! She realized that she had been looking for him, as well, on the rare occasions she had ventured into the London streets on some commission for Lady Bracken.

"Granted, her ladyship might not have recognized her own cousin in the description I gave. Few females would see one of their relations as the most beautiful blonde lady to appear in town in years."

"Good heavens," murmured Dora, reinterpreting in her mind her cousin Maud's surliness on the day after that theatre visit. Dora was afraid she might be colouring up under Carruthers's eyes. Was he engaging her in the kind of light flirtation she might expect from any man, or did his compliments mean something? Dora had spent too long out of the social scene to know how to classify his manners.

Sir Giles had been peering at the two in amusement. Now he cleared his throat.

Carruthers, recalling the presence of his friend, turned from Dora at last. "Well, old fellow, this charming lady isn't your daughter. Where is Miss Bracken, then?"

There was no need for Sir Giles to point his daughter out, for the dance had just ended and Augusta was being escorted back to her chaperone. The young lady's father vanquished her young partner, and when the unlucky ensign had turned his back, Augusta was presented to Carruthers.

Augusta blushed with pleasure at the introduction. "I believe we're acquainted with some connections of yours in Surrey, sir," she said boldly, looking up at the tall gentleman who seemed almost twice her size. "A Mrs. Farley and her family."

Dora tilted her head to one side. What could this gentleman have to do with Augusta's secret love, Edgar Farley?

Carruthers solved this mystery with his next words. "Ah, yes, my heir and his womenfolk. I trust you left them well."

"Oh, extremely well," said Sir Giles, with a sidelong look at his daughter. "The Farley boy's your heir then, Carruthers? Didn't know of the connection."

"Mr. Farley is such a worthy young man," Augusta stated, ignoring her father's frown.

"I'm sure he is. In orders, I believe? Must write to them soon," said Mr. Carruthers with a bored expression.

Dora was somewhat surprised to note that this casual and uncaring attitude toward the Farleys didn't stop Augusta from continuing to stare at Carruthers in a starry-eyed way. Could the child be infatuated with the man? And on a moment's acquaintance? A young girl could easily be taken in by a handsome face.

Dora's ruminations were cut short when Mr. Carruthers addressed her with a smile and another bow. "Miss Thornfield, may I have the pleasure of the next dance? I hope you waltz, but if you've not yet been to Almack's I'll be satisfied with the promise of a quadrille."

Dora smiled and returned, "Sir, when the patronesses of Almack's first saw me, the waltz hadn't yet come in. But in any case I must decline. I'm here only to chaperone Miss Bracken."

The gentleman's eyebrows flew up. "But if I insist?"

At this point Augusta burst in with her accustomed lack of delicacy. "Oh, nonsense, Dora, you must dance."

"Child, my dancing days are over," responded Dora with what she thought was a very mature air of resignation.

Sir Giles entered the fray. "Come, come, m'dear, if a pretty woman like you says her dancing days are over, what are some of those old frights doing out on the floor?" he said rather too loudly, provoking indignant looks from under several nearby turbans. Noticing this, the baronet coughed and continued in a softer voice, "As one might call me *your* chaperone, I advise you to go with Carruthers."

"You see, Miss Thornfield, we are all determined to carry our point," said Carruthers. He offered his arm, and not knowing how else to resist, Dora let him take her to the floor.

As it happened, Dora hadn't waltzed in public before. The shocking new dance hadn't been allowed at the country assemblies and private parties which had been her only recreation since her London season. She had never been gladder of the silly extravagance which had led her to call in a dancing master, shortly before her papa's death, that she might learn the steps of the craze which was sweeping London.

Mr. Carruthers was an excellent dancer. Dora matched his steps with ease as he guided her about the floor. On the rare occasions when she dared to look up into his eyes, she found him smiling at her in the strangely intimate way which she had noticed the only other time she'd seen him.

"Is something amiss, sir?" she finally asked.

"Oh, no," returned the gentleman, executing a difficult turn, which Dora managed to follow with slightly breathless precision. "I was merely congratulating myself on having found you. I'd begun to think the lovely blonde lady in Albemarle Street was a vision out of a dream."

Dora smiled. She couldn't help being pleased with such a compliment. But she didn't know what to say in return. She could hardly admit that she felt the same about him!

"I wonder, do you converse as well as you dance?" continued her partner.

"I'll assume that to be a compliment and answer with all due modesty that I have no idea," said Dora with an embarrassed laugh. "But I do have more experience in that art than that of the waltz."

"Indeed?"

"Yes. This is my first waltz, you see, unless I count the dancing master," confided Dora.

"Miss Thornfield, I consider this a signal honour. Is there anything else you might not have done before that I might assist you in? Any other dance, I mean."

"Sir!" Dora's eyes opened wide. He couldn't mean... She looked into his laughing face and was suddenly certain that his words did have a risqué intent. She countered by giving him a reproving glare and confining her responses to his questions to demure half smiles for the rest of the waltz. She enjoyed both the dance and the banter more than she cared to admit.

On the sidelines, the cats were as busy interpreting Dora's dance as was Dora herself. The object of Mr. Carruthers's choice—and Mr. Carruthers hardly ever danced—was soon identified as a cousin of the Brackens, actually Lady Bracken's companion! It was then pointed out that the lady had made quite a respectable appearance in town many seasons ago—*many* seasons. The wonder was that she hadn't married, for hadn't Sir John Webberley been after her? She was quite *passée* now, poor thing, though still in tolerable looks.

Perhaps Carruthers knew the gossips had their eyes on him and sought to confound them. He certainly succeeded, for his next choice as a partner was little Augusta Bracken. He had never been known to stand up with a white-gowned young slip of a thing in her first season. The fact that the child was hardly a beauty made this strange occurrence even more intriguing. It was impossible that the dance was other than a courtesy to the young girl's family, whispered the dowagers, for Carruthers was elusiveness personified, and the world had long given up on his marrying; but stranger matches had been made, and chits just out of the school-room were sometimes sought out by rakish older men as trainable and complaisant wives.

Back in her chair, Dora half attended to the remarks of Sir Giles's, who had not gone off to the card room at all, but observed Mr. Carruthers and her little cousin with quite as much attention as the gossips were bringing to the task. Augusta was blushing, half stumbling in confusion, prat-tling nonstop, and exhibiting other unmistakable signs of a girl falling in love. As for Carruthers, he seemed interested indeed in the girl's conversation. She even made him laugh! It was hardly likely that he would court such a young girl seriously. Was it? Dora frowned, and thought that if such an impossible thing should happen, it was even less likely that such a nonpareil as Carruthers would have any trouble in cutting out his heir, a poor boy from the country.

Dora was still frowning over this mystery when a crea-ture in blue gauze came floating over to rest on the chair next to hers. The lady was none other than Amelia, Lady Lavenham, Dora's dearest friend and old schoolmate. The two had met but once since Dora had been in London, thanks to Miss Thornfield's constant attendance upon Lady Bracken and stubborn refusal to be seen at most parties.

Lady Lavenham said a word to Sir Giles, then turned and devoted herself entirely to Dora. "You wicked creature, you never told me you were going out to balls now. You'll have no excuse to avoid mine when I give it, now will you?''

Dora repeated the oft-told tale of how she was only present as a chaperone.

"My dear, that won't wash. I saw you dancing with Mr. Carruthers. A handsome devil, isn't he? The alternate hope and despair of the matchmaking mamas for years now. It's quite a feather in your cap. His mother was Lady Anne Osmore, you know. And though there isn't a title, he's rich as a rent-lord. Most extraordinary, for Mr. Carruthers hardly ever dances anymore, and never with strangers. But perhaps you know him? Isn't he your friend, Sir Giles?'' Amelia looked up at the baronet.

"Yes, but he didn't know Cousin Theodora," said Sir Giles with his sardonic smile. "In fact, he thought she was my daughter."

Amelia's charming laugh rang out. "Quite a compliment, upon my word," she trilled with a sly look at Dora. Then, she bent her auburn head closer to Dora's blonde one and whispered, "I must warn you the man has his little interests. At the moment he's keeping a creature who's all the fashion. A very buxom dancer who does attitudes in the style of poor Lady Hamilton's. Derivative, but they go down rather well. She did a command performance at Carlton House only last week."

"Ah, you must mean Mademoiselle Yvette," put in Sir Giles.

"Sir! How could you mention such a name in the presence of ladies?" cried Amelia. She gave him a wink, and a mocking tap on the arm with her fan. "I was only warning Dora what she's up against."

Dora tried to look severe. "Are you really suggesting I set up to rival a Cyprian, Amelia?"

"You know I'm not. Well, I must go for now, dear, but I'll look for you later. And none of this talk about not dancing! Do you see to it, Sir Giles!" And, with another gay laugh and a flutter of blue gauze, Lady Lavenham moved on.

Dora didn't have long to mull over Amelia's speech, for she was almost immediately approached by a gentleman who asked her to dance. As she had done so once, and with so conspicuous a figure as Mr. Carruthers, she could hardly refuse. She was soon quite forgetting her dignified pose as chaperone to join in the evening's pleasures with as much enthusiasm as any debutante in the place.

"DEAR LADY, I will be desolated if you don't sit out at least one dance with me," said Sir James Perry an hour later, leaning forward so far that Dora was certain that her décolletage, not her face, was the true object of his interest. A stocky, grey-haired man with, as Augusta had just whispered, a very red nose, he had been plaguing Dora for fifteen minutes with very bold attentions.

"Sir, you mustn't tease Miss Thornfield out of her very real obligation to those of us who long to stand up with her. Your dancing days may be over, as I've heard you declare time and again, but I assure you mine are not," protested Captain Thomas Laughton.

Dora looked up at the latter gentleman in gratitude. The captain, Lady Vining's brother, was already proving a true friend. He was a young man of about Dora's age, and his golden hair and dancing blue eyes endeared him to many ladies, as did the faint aura of distinction that clung about him due to his bravery the year before in defence of the château of Hougoumont. In addition to these attractions, the captain was respectably wealthy. During the past interval Amelia had flitted up to Dora again, to recount the number of Thomas Laughton's acres in Yorkshire. There were also expectations from a crusty old uncle, General Sir Percival Laughton. Dora might see the general if she would but crane her neck a little toward the refreshment table.

"Heavens, Amelia, Captain Laughton danced with me once, he didn't propose," Dora had laughed, declining the treat of staring at the rich old general. Then she had had to look away in confusion as Amelia poked her playfully in the ribs, for Captain Laughton was approaching her again across the floor, with a flattering light of admiration in his eyes.

Dora had refused to give him two dances, and he had responded by staying to talk with her, undeterred when they were joined by Sir James Perry, baronet and desperate hunter for a stepmother to his houseful of "motherless little ones." Presuming on a slight acquaintance with Sir Giles to get an introduction to Dora, Sir James had immediately cornered her and confessed the size of his hopeful family, as well as their crying need of a good woman's care.

In fact, thought Dora as her two companions continued to banter, a comparison with Sir James made Captain Thomas Laughton seem almost indecently attractive. And he was obviously interested in her, a genteelly poor companion—for she had qualified Sir Giles's description of "cousin" to all comers by adding, "and Lady Bracken's companion."

Why, then, was she not more excited by the captain's distinguishing her?

She could think of one reason. Her eyes easily found the tall, commanding figure of Lawrence Carruthers. He was chatting with Augusta again, not ten feet from the place where Dora stood with her two cavaliers. Carruthers's fine head was thrown back in laughter at something the child was saying, and Dora strained her ears to hear, telling herself

that it was her duty to keep a short rein on Augusta.
Carruthers seemed to be calling the child a "devious little
creature," while Augusta modestly cast down her eyes. Now
what could that mean?

As Dora thought this over, Carruthers met her eye. His
gaze flickered over each of the men by the lady's side; then
he lifted his hands in a gesture of helplessness as he smiled
at Dora before turning back to his conversation with
Augusta.

"And now, dear lady, may I persuade you to eat supper
with me?" Sir James Perry asked. "My daughters Caroline
and Alice will delight in furthering their acquaintance with
you." A heavy sigh escaped him. "Ah, so unfortunate the
dear girls have no mama to present them to society."

"Their aunt seems very capable," Dora said firmly, tearing herself away from her eavesdropping. "She must have
done a fine job with the girls, for they are both so well-
mannered and dressed in such good taste." She had already
decided that the best answer to make to such hints by Sir
James was to describe his family life back to him as perfect
in every way—without the addition of a stepmother.

"Then are you forgetting your prior promise to eat supper with me, Miss Thornfield?" Captain Laughton put in
with a wink.

Dora's shoulders relaxed. There had been no such promise, but the captain understood the problem very well. Out
of the corner of her eye she saw that Carruthers had parted
from Augusta and was heading for the door of the ballroom. Well, why should he not? He probably had other
parties to attend this evening.

"Of course I'll keep my promise, sir," she returned, giving the captain a grateful glance. "So sorry, Sir James."

IN THE CARRIAGE GOING HOME Augusta was in ecstasies over what she chose to think of as Dora's triumph. "My dear cousin," she said happily, "that handsome Captain Laughton was most attentive. Too bad he had to leave supper early because of his horrid old uncle. Mama says the general's behaviour is always disgusting, but he's so rich you may meet him everywhere. Besides, he's Lady Vining's uncle, too, so naturally she had to invite him."

Dora smiled in remembrance. In his cups, General Sir Percival did seem to be a handful. Supper had been well under way when a ruckus of some sort had drawn the guests' attention. It was soon revealed that General Laughton, sweet as a lamb in his sober state, had left that happy condition behind and pinched Lady Jersey! The captain had had to hurry to the old man's side and take him out, first explaining in an undertone to the amused Dora his uncle's unfortunate tendency to mistake every woman for a female of easy virtue once he had had too much to drink.

"What a shame you got stuck with horrid Sir James for the rest of supper," sighed Augusta.

Dora was glad that Sir Giles was sleeping in his corner of the coach.

"His daughters are my age, so he won't do," Augusta pursued in a businesslike tone.

Dora forebore to mention that to many minds, a titled fifty-year-old widower would be thought of as quite an eligible *parti* for a penniless spinster approaching thirty. She hoped Sir James would forget about her; but if he continued his pursuit, at least there wouldn't be the added discomfort of Augusta's promoting the match in some gauche and obvious way.

"Let's not talk of my affairs," suggested Dora. "Tell me instead how you liked your father's friend, Mr. Carruthers. I wasn't aware that Mr. Farley was anyone's heir."

"Oh, he is only the heir-at-law—if Mr. Carruthers doesn't have children of his own. Now there is a very kind gentleman," said Augusta decidedly. It was too dark inside the vehicle to determine whether her words were accompanied by a maidenly blush. "He's not as old as I expected from the way Edgar described him," she added.

Dora agreed that Carruthers was not tottering on the brink of the grave, and they dropped the subject. Mr. Farley's name was not mentioned again, though the young man's relationship to Carruthers had given Augusta a natural opening. Dora could not help wondering if that omission could have its source in the feelings Carruthers had stirred in Augusta. What young female could resist such a handsome, sophisticated gentleman?

Dora did not consider herself a young female. But she was still thinking of Carruthers the next morning. His powerful arm had guided her about the ballroom floor all night in her dreams.

CHAPTER FOUR

WITH HER EYES STILL DAZZLED from the ball, Dora found it difficult next day to slip back into her assumed role of lady's companion. She, Theodora Thornfield, had really danced again in London! As she put on a dark, matronly dress, bound up her blonde curls into a severe coronet of braids, surmounted this structure with a fresh white cap, and then surveyed the entire ghastly effect in her bedroom mirror, Dora couldn't help thinking better thoughts of the reflection she had seen there the night before. Surely she was meant to wear silk, not this drab serge, and dress her hair in last night's modish knot of curls! What, she wondered, making a face at her sedate image before she left the room, would Mr. Lawrence Carruthers say if he could see her in this guise?

A dash into the library, where she had left her work-bag, gave Dora the unexpected answer to her question. Instead of being settled in the breakfast room, where any civilized head of a household should be at such an early hour, Sir Giles was leaning back in a leather chair entertaining a visitor. Dora could see no more of this latter than a pair of strong legs, encased in knit pantaloons and shiny Hessians, emerging from the chair that faced Sir Giles, but some instinct told her who the guest was. She started to back out of the room.

This plan was foiled when Sir Giles grinned and hailed her, and the other figure rose out of the chair.

"Miss Thornfield!" Carruthers, looking surprised, advanced to take her hand as she reluctantly stepped toward him. "What's become of my waltzing partner? Is a morning at the Bracken house usually a costume affair? If I'm not mistaken, that's a cap you have on."

Dora flushed. "This is my regular morning attire, sir," she returned in a stiff voice. She glared at him, and was further confused by the fun dancing in his hazel eyes.

"I won't argue with you as to the propriety of your headgear," the gentleman said, acknowledging defeat with a bow, "and on further observation, it doesn't mask your charms in the least." He had been holding on to her hand with both of his, and now he released it after what felt suspiciously like a caress.

"No use to spar with Cousin Theodora over the cap question. My daughter does it every day, and you see to what effect," Sir Giles put in. He opened the library door. "Carruthers, are you joining us for breakfast?"

Carruthers agreed to this, and the trio made for the parlour in question, Dora walking in the middle and wondering why, in heaven's name, she had chosen today to put on the oldest frock in her wardrobe. She would defend to the end her right to wear a cap, though; in a female of her age the stamp of spinsterhood was de rigueur. She knew Lady Bracken thought so, even if her outspoken daughter did not.

But she couldn't blame Mr. Carruthers for his remark. She herself had been lamenting the demise of the lovely lady in blue silk not two minutes earlier in front of her own mirror. Instead she sighed, regretting her lost youth as much as her present costume.

Mr. Carruthers directed a sharp look down at her. "Is something troubling you, ma'am?"

Dora, feeling very exposed, hastily denied that anything was.

Breakfast was laid out in a cheery parlour that got what morning light there was to be had in the precincts of Albemarle Street. The room was empty.

"Just as I thought," laughed Sir Giles. "My two ladies are still abed. Well, have a seat, Carruthers."

Dora was hesitating as Mr. Carruthers indicated that he would help her to a chair. "I'll go up to Lady Bracken," she said. "Perhaps she wants me to read the papers to her as she takes her chocolate."

"And perhaps she's still asleep. Sit down, Cousin Theodora." Sir Giles's blue eyes were twinkling, and Dora had the feeling he was enjoying this immensely. Sir Giles must know that Lady Bracken never did desire anyone's presence before she had emerged from the morning sulks with the aid of her abigail and a pot of strong chocolate. And did he also know that Dora, uncomfortable under Mr. Carruthers's amused, speculative eye, was both reluctant and anxious to leave the room?

In any case, she had no choice but to take the chair Mr. Carruthers was holding for her. She was soon sipping her coffee while the gentlemen's hearty appetites did justice to the array of fried meats, kippers and curried eggs spread upon the sideboard, the men talking of this and that old acquaintance.

"And are you enjoying the season, Miss Thornfield?" Mr. Carruthers turned his attention to the silent lady during a pause in Sir Giles's account of a Major somebody, gone to the bad.

Dora jumped. "The season? Oh, I see you mistake the matter, sir. I'm not the Brackens' guest, I'm..." She paused, realizing that Carruthers was not one of the gentlemen she had confessed this to the night before. "I'm Lady Bracken's companion. And Miss Bracken's chaperone," she added to explain her presence at the Vining ball.

Carruthers lifted an eyebrow. "Ah! That makes clear what I thought a rather zealous desire to read to her ladyship at this hour of the morning." He smiled, quite as warmly as before. A glance passed between him and Sir Giles, and Dora, noticing this, surmised that the two gentlemen would discuss her history at some future date, if Carruthers remembered to ask. She was certainly not about to go into it at the breakfast table, but she wouldn't be at all displeased if Sir Giles should reveal that his wife's cousin had come down in the world. The days of Thorne Park and prosperity were receding very quickly in Dora's memory, but she still had enough pride left to remind her that she had, indeed, belonged at last night's ball in a way few other paid companions could have claimed.

The conversation went on to other things, and breakfast wound to an end. Dora had very little to do with the conversation, but this suited her, for she was feeling unsure of her reception in the aftermath of her confession that she worked for a living. Carruthers had already begun a speech of leave-taking when the door burst open and Lady Bracken stood revealed on the threshold, her daughter hovering behind her.

Augusta, who looked very sleepy, was attired in what Dora recognized as her newest and most expensive morning gown, one of figured muslin, direct from the Bruton Street establishment of a leading couturière. Another creation of that modish house was draped about the elegant figure of Cousin Maud, whose bright dark eyes were now turned with avid interest on Mr. Carruthers.

"Oh, dauntless warrior," Sir Giles muttered into his plate.

His lady flashed him an irritated look, but she chose to ignore the remark. "How lucky that my abigail told me you had called, Mr. Carruthers," she cried, sweeping across the room to greet the gentleman. "It seems years since I saw you. So naughty of you to call only upon Sir Giles. But now that you've met my daughter, how charming of you to come to see her. Sweet Augusta—make your curtsey to Mr. Carruthers, dear—was telling me only a moment ago that you danced with her at the ball last night. I was so desolated that my wretched health wouldn't let me attend."

Carruthers bowed over the lady's hand. "Your deputy, Miss Thornfield, was well able to chaperone your charming daughter, ma'am." He acknowledged Augusta's presence with a nod, and Augusta returned an elfin smile; its air of intimacy surprised Dora.

"Oh! Cousin Theodora is quite capable," Lady Bracken answered. "Augusta, sit down." She did so herself, at one end of the table, motioning her daughter to the chair beside Mr. Carruthers, and the gentleman, forced out of politeness to remain awhile longer, resumed his seat.

"Snared!" murmured Sir Giles, looking innocently into the distance.

"What a charming attention, to call upon Augusta the morning after dancing with her. Such a gallant custom. Though if it were adhered to generally, I vow this house would be full to bursting with young men, for if I do say so myself, my Augusta has been causing quite a stir since her debut."

Lady Bracken chattered on. Dora was amused but not surprised by her ladyship's inattention to strict veracity, for if Augusta had caused even a ripple upon the social waters, it was news to her.

"Oh, Mama," protested Augusta with a blush.

"Now, now, my child, false modesty is no virtue," retaliated Lady Bracken in light, gay tones.

Augusta turned an impassive look on her mother. "Perhaps you do me too much credit, Mama. Mr. Carruthers obviously called to see Papa. Or perhaps he was paying his respects to Dora, for he also danced with her, you know.''

Lady Bracken had no response to make to this and merely stared. But her eyes were turned in the direction of her companion, and she did not look pleased.

A silence fell as Lady Bracken digested her daughter's pointed remarks. Then she resumed her bright smile, for Mr. Carruthers, in answer to Augusta's speculations, was making the only response possible.

''Why, Miss Bracken, how could you doubt that at least one of the objects of my call here today was to see how you did?'' he said with a wink. This boldness delighted the mother, for it suggested a quite friendly footing, and it didn't appear to disconcert Augusta, who merely smiled.

At that moment the butler entered the room, bearing a salver. Two cards with turned-down edges reposed upon the tray.

Lady Bracken caught them up. ''Captain Thomas Laughton and Sir James Perry,'' she read. ''How delightful! Lady Vining's brother is such a dashing young man.'' She shot a conspicuous look at her daughter. ''And the baronet—I suppose he wishes to see you, Sir Giles?''

Her ladyship's puzzled frown, as she tried in vain to consider a middle-aged widower as a probable suitor of her daughter's, provoked amusement in every other mind at the table. Dora exchanged a glance with Augusta and was sorry she had, for the young lady was hovering dangerously near a fit of the giggles.

''I'm certain Sir James does have particular business with someone in the house,'' Sir Giles answered his wife, with a placid smile.

Dora reddened. She might have known that Sir Giles had observed the assault Perry had made on her the night before.

Lady Bracken said, "Greaves, put the gentlemen in the drawing room and we will join them there. Mr. Carruthers, can you stay a little longer?" Her eyes gleamed almost fiercely. The idea of watching two rival suitors for Augusta's hand was admittedly intriguing.

The general remove to the drawing room began. "Oh, Cousin Theodora," Lady Bracken said casually, watching as Mr. Carruthers held that young woman's chair, "there's no need for you to go with us. My maid is laying out my lace ball gown, and you know you were good enough to say you'd help her mend the tear in it. My cousin's needlework is so exquisite," Lady Bracken informed Mr. Carruthers keenly, "and she is always so obliging."

Mr. Carruthers objected. "Ah, but the lady is also a charming addition to any company, and you shouldn't deny your callers the pleasure of her society."

"But I'd be delighted to mend your lace, Cousin Maud," Dora put in. "How shatterbrained of me not to have thought of it, and I did promise Meeker I'd show her my technique this morning. Good day, Mr. Carruthers."

Dora mounted the stairs as though she were pursued by the furies, nodding off the protests of Augusta and Sir Giles, which, added to those of Mr. Carruthers, made her feel pleasantly in request. Lady Bracken's order had really been a godsend, for Dora was extremely reluctant to expose her spinsterish morning self to yet more gentlemen who had met her the night before. Had they really come, as she suspected, to see her? In a way it was a shame not to find out in person, but that wish was nothing compared to the image of Lady Bracken, furious at her paid companion's putting herself forward to the extent of having gentlemen callers.

DORA MADE VERY QUICK WORK of the lace-mending project and then ensconced herself in her room, where she changed to a prettier cap and re-did her hair in case she should be called to the drawing room. She didn't go so far as to change her gown, but she was guilty of filling in the square neckline of the drab brown garment with a scarf of fine Mechlin lace. Then, assuring herself that her presence would certainly not be required that morning, she sat perched on the edge of a chair and pretended to read Goldsmith's *History of England*, which improving work she had promised herself to get through before she was much older.

In spite of herself she grew engrossed in the house of York and lost track of time; and she was just rousing herself to begin a letter to one of her sisters when there was a peremptory tap at the door and Lady Bracken's dresser peeked in.

"You're to go to her ladyship now, ma'am, in her boudoir."

Dora looked up. "Thank you, Meeker," she said with a cheerful nod, putting the book aside.

Lady Bracken had arranged herself regally in a deep chair by the window. "Ah, Cousin. Do come in. Heavens, what use is it to have a companion if you're never with me?"

Dora approached and drew a small chair up to face her employer. She didn't bother to mention that it was by her ladyship's own orders that she had left her side.

"Are the callers gone, then?" she asked.

Lady Bracken emitted a deep, rattling sigh. "My word, those gentlemen were so very strange, Cousin Theodora! I'm extremely flattered, for my girl's sake, that those two men of property and distinction are rivals for her affection—and her in town only a month!—but they would keep sparring with each other for the length of the call. Which only goes to prove," she added with a shrewd look at her companion, "that they do both have tendres for Augusta."

"Captain Laughton and Mr. Carruthers, you mean?" queried Dora innocently. Perhaps—her heart sank a little at the thought—both men were indeed Augusta's admirers. Captain Laughton had danced with the girl at the ball, too.

"Yes, whoever else would I mean, my dear?" Lady Bracken was answering a touch impatiently. Her expression cleared and she shook her head playfully at Dora. "But you didn't tell me, Theodora, that you had picked up a cavalier at the Vinings'. How very sly! And though I can't really approve of a lady in your situation putting herself forward in quite the way you must have done to attract his notice, I will concede that if you were to marry Sir James Perry it would be the coup of the season. He's such a respectable man. Greaves omitted to mention it, but Sir James brought his daughters along today. Augusta gets on with them famously. Nonsense to bring them out together, but Sir James, being a man, can't be expected to know what's proper. It will be different when he has a wife by his side." And Lady Bracken fairly leered at Dora. "Had I known how things stood, my sweet, I certainly would have had you in to the drawing room. Sir James asked after you particularly, and so did Miss Perry and Miss Alice. The dear girls love you already. And I believe there are at least seven more little Perrys at home."

Dora dropped her eyes and hid a quiet shudder at the thought of such a large family under her care. "Oh, Cousin Maud, I'm certain Sir James does not—"

"And I, my dear, am just as certain that he does. Don't worry about leaving us when the time comes. Though it will be inconvenient to have to replace you, I won't deny my own cousin the chance to settle herself in such a respectable fashion."

The repetition of that word made Dora feel bent already under the heavy weight of Sir James's attentions. She was glad she hadn't gone down to the drawing room.

Lady Bracken was continuing. "When I saw that you had indeed found an admirer suitable to your age and situation, my dear, I decided not to speak to you as strongly as I might have otherwise on the subject of the embarrassing way you threw yourself at Mr. Carruthers's head. Oh, I grant you the gentleman is handsome, my love, but he's all but declared himself for Augusta. And I, for one, can think of nothing more pathetic than a spinster making clumsy attempts to fix the interest of such a man."

Dora choked in amazement. "Cousin Maud, I assure you that at no time did I throw myself at his head! Good heavens!" Her normally mild eyes flashed, and she stood up. "I'll leave tomorrow. When I agreed to become your companion, Cousin, I made up my mind to a certain amount of discomfort, but this passes all bounds. And as for Augusta's prospects, do remember that Mr. Carruthers met her only last night. Good day, ma'am. I will be packing my things if you should have need of me." And Dora turned on her heel and marched out of the room toward an inescapable life of rural solitude in the houses of her sisters. Her cheeks were burning. Her only chance at a kind of independence, and she hadn't been able to humble herself at the first sign of trouble! The sneaking feeling that she did, indeed, have a certain admiration for Lawrence Carruthers didn't alter her sense of outrage and ill-use. She hadn't put herself forward at all! If anyone had taken a step toward furthering an acquaintance, it had been the gentleman.

"Cousin Theodora! Do come back," cried Lady Bracken. "Whatever would Sir Giles say? Upon reflection, of course you must not have made any overtures to Mr. Carruthers. He doubtless only asked you to dance last night as a courtesy to the family. I— Oh, Cousin, do turn round!"

Dora heard the pleading note in Lady Bracken's voice and did look back. She had been useful to her Cousin Maud, she knew that very well. In the weeks that she had been with the family, she had shepherded Augusta on shopping tours, thus saving the young lady's mama many a boring trip; she had fetched this and carried that; and most importantly she had been an audience, for Lady Bracken's daughter and husband scarcely even made the pretence of listening to her. Dora not only sat through the longest monologue, she kept up a running murmur in imitation of interest.

And what *would* Lady Bracken tell Sir Giles, who in the short time of their renewed acquaintance had developed a sincere respect for a young woman he had formerly known only as a giddy young debutante?

It was almost worth forty years spent wiping the noses of her sisters' children to cause an uproar in the Bracken family; for Dora had no very sincere affection for her cousin Maud. Lady Bracken had been an adequate young lady's chaperone when Dora had spent that long-ago season in her house, but as the mistress of a paid companion she was frequently unbearable.

"Cousin," wheedled Lady Bracken, applying a handkerchief to a dry eye.

Dora gave over. "I know you didn't mean it," she said. "If you'll forgive my little outburst, I'll forget what you said. And, Cousin Maud, I really must beg you not to run on about me and Sir James. I don't like the man! And I don't want to marry him."

Lady Bracken, restored to humour in a flash, let out a trill of laughter. "Ah, Cousin Theodora, you learned your lessons well. A young lady must never show interest too soon, so I've told my Augusta time and again, and that good advice applies to a lady past her youth as well. Why should it not? But I'll say nothing more," she added in haste, seeing Dora's black look. "Now do be a dear and fetch the morning post. I saw an intriguing stack of invitations lying on the hall table as I came upstairs, but I didn't stop to pick them up. I knew you'd be so good.''

Dora, with difficulty refraining from tugging an imaginary forelock, hastened about her business. Sir Leonard Fitzhugh's warnings about the difficulties of a paid post were thundering in her ears. This life was certainly nothing like independence! But at least, Dora thought grimly, she was earning her way.

CHAPTER FIVE

WHEN THE MOST FASHIONABLE Cyprian in London breaks up with her lover, a scene is necessary. Such was the reflection of the famous dancer, Mademoiselle Yvette—she admitted to no other name—as she wound herself up for the pièce de résistance.

"Monstre!" she shrieked, striking a pose in the middle of her pink-and-gold boudoir. *"Diable! Séducteur!"* She grabbed the nearest object to hand and let it fly.

Lawrence Carruthers neatly dodged the cloisonné bowl and allowed a laugh to escape him. "Seducer? Don't let your dramatics overcome your good sense, my dear."

Yvette, in the act of aiming a statuette of Bacchus at a certain aristocratic nose, had the grace to pause and smile through her histrionic tears. No, the part of injured innocent was no longer hers to play. Though she had been no more than a child when she had been chosen from the opera ballet by her first protector, that had been some twenty years ago. She and Carruthers were of an age, though she would have died rather than admit to it.

"But to leave me without so much as a word, and for no reason—it is infamous!" she pursued, replacing the smile instantly with the stormiest expression that flashing dark eyes and petulant carmined mouth could manage. She tossed her unbound hair, a rich tangle of raven curls that had always been her pride.

Carruthers shrugged. "My love, this is your word. And if it comes to reasons, you've no doubt done something to cause me to cut the connection. Our agreement did specify constancy, you'll recall, and there have been rumours... you understand me."

Yvette looked indignant, but said nothing. Her brief liaisons with every young man who caught her eye were legend. Long ago, when she had been younger and more foolish, she had actually turned her back on more than one protector to run off with a footman or impoverished actor. She was wiser now, canny enough to hang on to a rich man of the ton while indulging her more plebeian tastes behind closed doors. Yes, she was very discreet. That was why it infuriated her so that this latest gentleman was decamping out of the blue. What reason had she given him? His veiled allusions to infidelity were completely unfounded, for she had been more than careful. Yvette's fingers, curled around the china Bacchus, itched to fling it in the handsome face that was surveying her with such insolent amusement.

"Dresden, I believe. It would bring a pretty penny if you let it live," remarked Carruthers. His hand was on the gilt door handle. "There is nothing personal in this decision of mine, you know."

"*Oui,* so you said. The insult! Nothing personal! The good God protect me!" Yvette, changing tactics, set the Bacchus down on the table and flung herself onto the nearest chaise longue for a bout of noisy sobbing.

Carruthers had a flash of guilt, for though he doubted very much that his mistress had any attachment to him, his leave-taking of her had been colder than necessary. He suspected he had been unchivalrously paying her back in kind for some of the French pragmatism which was wont to follow Yvette behind the bed curtains and which, though only to be expected from the muslin company, was never flattering. He approached the chaise and ran his fingers over the raven curls, a light touch only to forestall any thoughts of a reconciliation. "My dear, I've simply come to the point in my life where I no longer wish to keep a mistress."

Yvette looked up. "How is that? There can be no such time! No, I know men. You've contracted with someone else. If it's that horrid creature they call the Mockingbird, I'll rip the doxy's hair from her head, I swear it!"

Sitting down beside the distraught woman and noticing that, even in her anger, she had arranged her opulent, silk-clad curves in the most enticing pose possible, Carruthers said gently, "I have no new candidate for your position, *ma chère*. But perhaps I'm thinking of marriage."

"Bah! Never before have I had an *unmarried* protector! That is no reason." Yvette sniffled delicately into a lace pillow. But her dark eyes, still bright with tears, grew thoughtful. "Ah, you mean we should be discreet for the nonce, so that this schoolroom miss you are to wed will not be shocked by the gossip? I comprehend."

Carruthers laughed. "How quickly you develop an entire story around a single comment. My marriage is no settled thing, and the...lady in the case not so easily classified. But I mean to reform, and keeping you—and you are very famous, my dear, make no mistake—would not put me high in the esteem of any respectable female."

As Carruthers knew, Yvette had no very good opinion of "respectable females" and would not be insulted by such a statement. She was not; in fact, she seemed to preen a little at the allusion to her fame. She had had her ups and downs in her career, and to have come about in such a way—to be at the very pinnacle of success at an age when most women were on their way out—was something.

"So it's my luck that's brought about my undoing?" Yvette rose to a sitting position and smiled through her tears. Her chin jutted out, and she looked the picture of brave beauty. A white hand covered in rings caressed Carruthers's cheek. "*Eh bien.* If things don't go well for you in this marriage project, or even if they do, I will be here. Remember that, *chéri.*"

Carruthers smiled rather cynically and patted the hand. He got up and moved to the door, wondering a little at his ladybird's sudden mildness. Best to make good the escape before a worse mood overtook her. "Good luck, Yvette," he said before he went out. Taking his leave of a Cyprian always embarrassed him.

Mounting up into his curricle outside Yvette's door, he made his way into the city, where he arranged with his man of business the proper provision for his mistress's future. The lease of the house in Charles Street for the sixmonth more it had to run, and a generous gift of money. Yvette should be pleased.

Lawrence Carruthers knew he was. He had been planning to end his colourful but tiresome affair with Yvette for weeks—or was it months?—but had delayed simply because he had no one to replace her. He still didn't, but his thoughts were turning these days to a woman who would be more than a bed partner. Surprising and unprecedented dreams of marriage had been spinning through his head in the past few days. The project was only in the first stages, but Carruthers had hopes.

So, had he but known it, did Yvette. As the door closed behind her former protector, the hand of the *danseuse* had curled itself into a fist. So he thought he could shake her off as if she were no more than a speck of dust on his coat?

Yvette had been harbouring a secret within her bosom for some time now. She was at the very peak of her career as a Cyprian and had nowhere to go but down. What better way to save herself than to marry? Carruthers was rich and his own master. He was untitled, true, but that was an advantage, for marriage to a doxy would raise the hackles of an aristocratic family. Yvette had done her research. Carruthers was highly connected on his mother's side, but his father's people were mere untitled gentry. What was to stop him from pleasing himself in his choice?

Yvette had supplemented her enquiries into Carruthers's business with some very important hours spent before her own mirror. Lines about the eyes, a white strand or two in the famous raven hair, had led her to take this decision while the taking was good. She had fancied that dear Laurent, as she called him, would not be easily talked round to her way of thinking. The task would be difficult but not impossible, a true challenge to Yvette's famous powers of persuasion. She sighed, remembering his touch. She was a practical woman making a cold decision to secure her future, but she had to admit there were more than economic advantages to her plan. What a lover he was! That detail made the prospect of matrimony quite appealing.

And now to be done out of this happy plan by a silly chit! Yvette had no doubt her rival was a schoolroom miss, pushed at Carruthers by some devious dowager from the ton. The wonder was that he would let himself be caught in such an insipid trap.

Yvette crossed to the window and, drawing back the gauzy pink curtain which filtered the sunlight in a way so flattering to the complexion, she watched Carruthers's curricle proceed down the street. He was not yet married, she must remember that. He had admitted that his plans were not settled.

The snapping Gallic eyes narrowed. The *première danseuse* of London was not without friends. There were those who owed favours to Mademoiselle Yvette. It would be easy to find out the identity of this respectable miss who had captured Lawrence Carruthers's imagination, if not his heart. And it should be child's play to win out over the green creature.

"GREAT NEWS!" trilled Lady Bracken, bursting into the morning room where her companion was sitting. Cousin Maud had dragged her daughter on a round of morning calls. Miss Thornfield's presence had not been required.

"News?" Dora looked up from her book. In her time with the Brackens she had learned to make the best use of her time alone, and reading was something she could not do while listening to the lady of the house.

Lady Bracken settled into a chair near the fire, removing her elaborate plumed bonnet as she did so, and unbuttoning her velvet pelisse. "I sent dear Augusta up to my room to fetch me a shawl, for I wanted to let you know what I heard, dear cousin, and it's not precisely fit for young, innocent ears."

Dora's eyes glinted in amusement. She had lately been daring to be a little satirical with her cousin. "As a respectable spinster, I'll concede that my ears are not young, but innocent? Ah, cousin, how could they be otherwise?"

"Theodora! How droll you are! You know I didn't mean . . . that is to say, naturally at your time of life you've heard, if not done, things Augusta still can't feature. Sweet, innocent child!" Lady Bracken paused to beam into the distance. "She little knows what a happy future awaits her."

"Yes. A happy future." Dora fingered the binding of her book, the third volume of a particularly engrossing novel, and wondered if she would be chided for forwardness if she simply demanded that her cousin come to the point.

"Well, I see you're dying to know what's happened, dear girl." Lady Bracken leaned forward and said in a half whisper, "I heard it at Lady Cowper's! It's all over the town that Carruthers has given his mistress her *congé*. Sure sign he's considering matrimony!''

''Carruthers!'' Dora's cheeks were suddenly burning, but this unhappy fact could be explained away as embarrassment at the shocking subject of the present conversation. ''But, Cousin Maud, gentlemen change mistresses every day. Why on earth should that become a subject of gossip in society?'' His mistress had been that famous dancer; yes, Amelia Lavenham had mentioned that. Dora had seen Carruthers several times in the past few days, and her fascination with him hadn't abated in the least. On the contrary, she was becoming obsessed with him, and she was intrigued by this insight into the gentleman's personal life. She felt a sudden, sharp stab of jealousy, though, thinking of the man in the arms of some gorgeous ladybird.

''Well, it's true that most gentlemen keep their little interests. I've been so lucky in that regard with dear Sir Giles, who wouldn't look at another woman. But you don't fully comprehend, my dear. It seems Carruthers had taken some trouble to have this news get about. He wishes the world to know he's become a reformed man. Now what could provoke that sort of behaviour but an interest in marriage to a certain young girl of our acquaintance? An innocent child who would be put off by what a more sophisticated woman might be expected to take in her stride?'' Lady Bracken's voice was complacent. She had quite made up her mind.

Dora had to concede that, if Carruthers had indeed taken care to make it known he was leaving off dealing with ladies of the evening, he must have a very good reason. She wondered what it really was.

Cousin Maud's voice was running on and on as she exulted over what she considered Augusta's latest coup. Dora frowned. Poor Mr. Carruthers! If he only knew that his every move was being considered a step toward a connec-

tion with Augusta Bracken! Dora suspected he would laugh.
Or . . . would he?

Every time Dora had seen him, he had had an intimate
smile and a flirtatious glance for her. And she still dreamed
of his arm about her waist during their waltz at the Vining
ball. But she had to admit that he was suspiciously friendly
with Augusta. He and the chit always laughed together, and
they made a habit of snatching a moment for a private
word.

Cousin Maud, for all her tendency to find a romance for
Augusta under every tall-crowned beaver hat in Mayfair,
might be right for once in her life. The scene the fond
mother was setting out was plausible. Carruthers, a bachelor approaching his middle years and probably wanting to
set up his nursery, might well decide on a rich young bride
who happened to be the daughter of an old friend. People
would be surprised by such a match, but not astonished.
And there was no evidence at all that such a gentleman
would ever consider, for more than a dance or a flirtation,
a penniless paid companion past her first youth.

Dora sighed. Lady Bracken halted her monologue to ask
if Cousin Theodora were suffering from the headache, and
Dora agreed, reluctantly, that such was the case. She could
think of no other good reason for her incautious sound of
distress, and she certainly didn't want to draw Cousin
Maud's fire again in the matter of Mr. Carruthers. It would
be quite as bad to be accused of pining for the man as of
angling for him!

"Well, Cousin, it must be all that reading you do in a bad
light. What can be keeping Augusta with my shawl? Do go
and hurry her along, my dear. The walk upstairs will do
your head the world of good. Air and exercise, that's what
Sir Giles always says when I complain of the migraine."

Dora rose, and Lady Bracken, by now divested of her outdoor things, put her feet up on the sofa. "Dear Augusta! Settled in her first season," she was murmuring contentedly as her cousin left the room.

On her way up to Lady Bracken's boudoir, Dora tried not to think of Mr. Carruthers and his affairs, and wondered by the way if she would ever get used to this life of running errands.

For some reason, when she came upon Augusta, dallying in the upper hall with Mama's shawl on her arm, she had to restrain herself from snapping at the innocent young thing.

"Have you heard news of your Mr. Farley lately, dear?" she made herself ask instead in a sweet voice, struggling to make her mood match.

Augusta started. "Oh. Edgar." There was a brief pause, and then she shrugged. "I must suppose he's well. Oh, Dora, have you heard the latest *on dit*? Mr. Carruthers had a mistress, a beautiful black-haired dancer, and he's given her up. Isn't that shocking?"

"Child, what would your mother say if she could hear you?" laughed Dora. "She just whispered that tidbit to me, as something not fit for your young ears."

"Oh! I'm not quite the milk-and-water miss Mama thinks me," said Augusta with a toss of her head, and the two descended to the sitting room and another afternoon of pretending to listen to Lady Bracken.

CHAPTER SIX

"FOR ME?"

"Yes, ma'am. They are downstairs in the hall."

Dora rose abruptly from the desk where she had been composing three nearly identical letters to her sisters. "Thank you, Betsy. I'll go right down."

The maid bobbed a slight curtsey and disappeared. Flowers! There were flowers down in the hall. Dora's heartbeat quickened, but even in her excitement an unworthy thought penetrated her brain. Had she not been a paid companion, Betsy would have carried the delivery up to her. There had been no malice in the girl's message, only an implicit realization of Miss Thornfield's place in the household, a knowledge which Miss Thornfield herself shared. And under the circumstances, Dora was pleased to go and fetch her property.

She made her way down the front stairs with a very quick step. It was years since she had received flowers. With every footfall she was telling herself that they could not be from Mr. Carruthers. He barely knew her. He was rumoured to be distinguishing Augusta (though Dora couldn't quite believe that). He had probably forgotten the very existence of Theodora Thornfield in the three days since he had called at the house....

On the hall table lay a modest bouquet of spring flowers: a few jonquils and irises in a simple paper holder. The quiet good taste of the gift enchanted Dora on sight. No one but

Mr. Carruthers, surely, could be so thoughtful, so sensitive to the delicate position she was in in this house—for Lady Bracken would certainly have something to say if she found out her companion had received a more noticeable gift, such as a basket of roses. A little thing like a few blossoms would probably not even come to her ladyship's ears; it had been perfectly thought out. Descending the last step, Dora ran to the table and snatched up the card that was tucked into the flowers. Her hand trembling a little, she read the name.

"Damnation!" she was guilty of saying in the next moment, luckily in a very low voice. Then, biting her lip in embarrassment at her strong language, Dora tucked the card into her pocket and snatched the bouquet from the table. Sir James Perry! Of all the irritating attentions. The innocent flowers suddenly changed from a sweet, consciously understated present, into the economical offering of a determined, but practical, widower. Dora would no doubt encounter the baronet soon, and have to thank him for distinguishing her. She hoped she'd be able to muster the proper iciness along with her thanks, and thus forestall his doing the same thing again.

"Is there something wrong, Miss Thornfield?" a voice enquired, and Dora whirled about to see Mr. Carruthers, of all people, striding down the hall toward her. He looked amused; perhaps he had heard Dora's profane outburst. "A spider in those flowers, perhaps?"

"Sir! Why, I was merely surprised by the gift," Dora answered. She had to return his smile, for it was so very warm and friendly, and it struck her as quite funny that thoughts of this man had somehow made him appear. Thank heaven the same couldn't be said of Sir James Perry!

"I'm very glad to see you," Carruthers was going on, continuing to smile and to eye Dora with what was either admiration or a very fair imitation. "I've just been visiting your cousins in the drawing room and was on my way out. I hope your headache's better?''

"My headache?'' Dora instantly grasped the reason Lady Bracken had allowed her this unprecedented morning of leisure to be passed in her own room. Mr. Carruthers had obviously been expected, and Cousin Maud was quite as evidently trying to keep him far away from her companion. Well, this was gratifying in a way, for Lady Bracken's eyes were sharp, and she must sense that in Dora her daughter had a kind of rival.

Dora's puzzled tone had told Mr. Carruthers what he wanted to know about her absence from the female gathering this morning. "Yes, your headache,'' he repeated, with a wink. "Really, my dear Miss Thornfield, you must learn to coordinate your excuses with the other members of the household. But I'll forgive you this lapse.''

"Will you, sir?'' Dora was beginning to enjoy this banter, and she looked up, laughing, into his eyes.

Carruthers caught his breath. Miss Thornfield's face, framed by the light curls that couldn't help escaping from that ridiculous little cap she affected, was truly lovely when lit by laughter, and her grey eyes were like stars above the flowers she held clutched to her breast. Who the devil was sending her flowers? "Yes,'' Carruthers answered in a more serious tone than the joking question warranted, "I will.''

They were standing in the hall, a narrow room enlivened by one or two good pictures and carpeted in a fine Axminster. Only the elegant Chippendale table, where the mail was put, and one or two hard chairs against the walls relieved its emptiness. But as if to make up for this paucity of furniture, a very solid, very real footman was standing just inside the door. He was at attention, Carruthers's hat and cane in his hand, waiting to see the visitor out. And, incidentally, observing all that should happen before that exit.

Carruthers flashed the man an irritated glance and drew Dora off to the far side of the hall, where he sat her down in a straight chair which was usually only warmed by some lady's maid waiting for her mistress, and took the seat next to her. "Too bad you missed my visit with the ladies," he said.

Dora, who had let herself be propelled as though under a mesmeric trance and was not best pleased by it, looked at him curiously. "My head, you know," she said in a sweet voice.

"You missed a most affecting scene," pursued the gentleman. "You might have witnessed my confessing past sins to your good cousin and her charming daughter, and assuring them that my habits have taken a turn for the better."

Dora stared. "I hardly dare to think you'd mention your, er, sins in front of a young girl, whatever they—the sins— might be," she said in a reproving tone. "My dear sir, you must remember that Augusta is only seventeen. Ah, but I see you're roasting me," she said, catching the twinkle in his eye, "and you haven't been doing any such thing." Naturally her mind leaped to the news Cousin Maud had picked up yesterday at Lady Cowper's. Carruthers had given up his mistress and was anxious for people to know it!

"My dear lady, you mustn't underestimate the extent of my boldness," Carruthers said, smiling even more broadly than before. "Nor the sincerity of my reform. Do we understand each other?"

"Not altogether," Dora stated. "What can your habits have to do with me? Naturally I'll publish news of your blameless life far and wide, if that's what you want of me. However—" she dared a significant, shrewd look into his face "—I hear you've enlisted society in that project already, for heaven knows what reason.''

Carruthers threw back his head and laughed, revealing strong white teeth and an endearing set of lines about the eyes. "Let a man be dissolute, and society's blasé about the matter,'' he said when his hilarity had wound down. "But have him take a turn for the better and the gossips have a field day. If you must know, Miss Thornfield, I was wishing to see if the ton would make much of my, er, reform. It seems I have my answer. Good Lord, isn't it an odd world? Amusing, but odd.''

"I can hardly believe you'd set yourself to being talked about merely to laugh over the result,'' Dora said severely, but she wondered if this simple reason didn't have the ring of truth which Lady Bracken's theories, and society's, seemed to lack.

Carruthers responded by favouring her with another wink. He seemed quite pleased with himself. Then his eyes lit on the blossoms Dora still clutched in her hands. "Well, ma'am, I've got out all my own poor secrets. Won't you reciprocate?''

Dora saw where he was looking. There was no reason to be reticent, so she said, with a little sigh, "Sir James Perry was kind enough to send me these. Though it's none of your affair, Mr. Carruthers,'' she felt bound to add. Her heart was singing, and she suddenly found it difficult to control her breathing. He cared that she was receiving flowers from another man! How promising, she might have said, if she had been an ordinary lady with a dowry and a secure place in society. As a spinster working for a living, she was still thrilled by such interest, but she didn't know how to classify it.

"Sir James Perry!" Carruthers was exclaiming with every appearance of hearty approval. "A very worthy man. A widower, I think, with a large and hopeful family?"

"Very large," Dora said, hiding a smile.

Carruthers looked even more satisfied. "Well, I can only admire the gentleman's taste. And now I must take leave of you, Miss Thornfield." He rose, and Dora got up with him. He bowed over her hand and kissed it, and Dora found herself shivering at the feel of his lips on her bare skin.

When the heavy oaken portal had closed behind Carruthers, Dora turned to take her flowers upstairs. But before she had quite lost sight of Silas, the footman, she was certain she saw the man give her a significant nod.

As the day went by, and Lady Bracken neither teased Dora about the flowers, nor chided her for conversing with Mr. Carruthers on the sly, Dora realized that neither Betsy, the maid, nor the footman were going to betray her secrets. How nice it was that she had somehow gained the loyalty of Lady Bracken's staff!

THE NEXT DAY, Dora was engaged to spend the morning with Amelia Lavenham. Amelia herself had wheedled permission for this luxury from Lady Bracken, stressing her own eagerness to talk over old times with Dora, and dropping significant names and half-promises of fine invitations in front of the baronet's lady like crumbs before a starving bird. Permission had been granted, for Lady Bracken saw no reason not to brag about her cousin's intimacy with the great hostess Lady Lavenham, and she could hardly do so if she never let Theodora go near the woman. Letting only one sigh over her unsorted embroidery threads escape her, she had told Dora to go and enjoy herself.

"Sweet creature," gushed Amelia as soon as she had got Dora alone in her elegant boudoir in Portman Square, "I've been perishing to ask you about all your beaux. How naughty of you to be so inaccessible. Really, you might have told me you wanted to come to town, and I'd have invited you as my guest, for as long a time as you wanted. Can't you still give up your little post and come to me? It would be so much more comfortable.''

"Well, Amelia, I've told you so often that I wanted to be independent and make my own way in the world that I won't waste time repeating myself," Dora replied, accepting the plate of sweet cakes Amelia held out to her and selecting two of the best. "And I'm too old to make a display of myself in London. It would be absurd to go about with you quite as if I had hopes of catching a husband." She looked down as she spoke the last words, conscious that she was being a little less than candid.

"Fustian!" Amelia exclaimed, confirming Dora's own secret opinion of her speech. "It's all over town that you've three on your string, even at your decrepit age. By the way, I'll thank you not to be proclaiming your ancientness to people born in your year."

Dora disregarded Amelia's playful complaint. "Three beaux?" she gasped.

"Do you mean to tell me there are more?" countered Amelia with a sly smile.

"Who are they supposed to be?" asked Dora.

"Well, Sir James Perry, for one. Everyone saw him fawning over you at the Vining ball, and he's been singing your praises ever since and saying how much he looks forward to seeing you at my ball. I saw the gentleman in Bond Street yesterday, in fact, and it was all 'dear Miss Thornfield' and 'such a sweet lady.' Oh the man's meaning is clear enough."

"What a wretched coil," sighed Dora. "He sent me flowers, you know."

"Sir James? But he's known for his penny-pinching," Amelia said, her blue eyes widening at this sign of the gentleman's ardour. "Heavens, he must be serious indeed. And you're not, I take it?"

"Amelia! How can you even think . . . !"

"Don't rip up at me, dear. How was I to know you might not welcome the care of a family? You'd be Lady Perry, and there'd be all those children. And a home of your own."

Dora shrugged. "If you must know, that's the worst of it. If Sir James should indeed offer for me, wouldn't it be my Christian duty to agree? His children do need care, and what else have I got to do with my life? The thought of marrying Sir James angers me the more for being such a sensible solution to my problem. I won't last out the year with Cousin Maud, you know. I'm not cut out for the companion role, at least not on an extended basis. I'll come to blows with her sooner or later, and it will be so deflating to have to go back to my sisters when that happens."

"But you can't care for Sir James," Amelia said, and Dora nodded.

"Well, who could?" Amelia continued in a bracing manner. "I say your other two suitors are much more agreeable, and Freddy thinks the same."

"And who are these mysterious two you and your husband find so agreeable?" Dora asked, making her eyes go wide, as though with curiosity.

"Captain Laughton, for one. A very nice man. So brave, too. The gentlemen tell me nothing but good things of his behaviour during the late unpleasantness. He's very fond of you."

"Because he danced with me a little at one ball?" Dora laughed. She had enjoyed the captain's attentions at the time, especially as they had meant such a welcome respite from Sir James, but she hadn't taken him seriously in the least.

"Well, he found out I was your old friend and called here the other day to positively catechize me about Miss Thornfield. So there!" Amelia nodded her bright head in pleased certainty. "And of course there's Lawrence Carruthers."

"Lawrence Carruthers?" Dora repeated in true distress. She had forgotten the gossip that was always rampant in society, even, it would seem, about such an insignificant personage as herself. "What in the world could make you jump to that conclusion?"

"Why, everything, dearest. Dancing with you at the ball, and a waltz at that! And people say he lost no time in shedding himself of that Yvette creature."

Dora shook her head. "Perhaps he was only tired of her. It never fails to amaze me that his leaving one mistress should be taken to mean that Carruthers is hanging out for a wife."

"Oh!" Amelia's eyes were sharp. "You'd heard of it."

"From the man himself, as it happens," Dora declared, deciding on the spot not to lie. "In very veiled terms, of course. And he told me he'd only made the situation known in order to have a laugh at society's expense. And he must be having it. Amelia, you surely haven't told anyone that his purpose in getting rid of—Yvette, was it?—had to do with me? Nothing could be further afield. Why, Lady Bracken is certain that Carruthers is planning to marry Augusta, and he took this puritanical turn for fear of offending the child."

Amelia shrugged. "I'd be very surprised if Carruthers married that little chit."

"The chit's mama will be shocked if he does not," Dora retorted, wishing she were as certain as Amelia that Carruthers had no serious interest in Augusta.

Well, only time would give the answer to that mystery, and Dora's purpose now must be to dissuade Amelia from littering the ton with references to her friend's "conquest." Eventually, Amelia promised, but Dora couldn't seem to erase that silly gleam from Lady Lavenham's eye. By the time she returned to Albemarle Street, Miss Thornfield's head was awhirl as she imagined married life with Sir James Perry (never, unless death or disgrace were the only alternatives), Captain Laughton (what a shame it was that such a nice, handsome man could not inspire one flutter in Dora's bosom!) and Mr. Lawrence Carruthers (impossible! He, with his looks and breeding, might marry where he wished, and aim much higher than a penniless companion!)

"FREDDY, I'LL SEE DORA well married by the end of the season or know the reason why," Amelia Lavenham said that evening, speaking in the loud tones she had to use to travel down the long table to her husband's end.

"Is that so, m'dear?" was Lord Lavenham's bored response.

"Our ball will be the perfect place to begin my campaign," Amelia continued with a martial glitter in her eye.

"Ball's as good a place as any," rejoined her husband, draining his wineglass.

"There are nothing but balls all the wretched season," Amelia sighed. "But my parties are always the best—everyone says so. And this year I shall have the satisfaction of knowing I set my dearest friend on the road to happiness. The sort of happiness you and I have, Freddy, my love."

Lord Lavenham's answer to this was extremely satisfying. His languor disappeared as he rose from his chair, made his way down the long dining room and clasped his wife in his arms. Amelia melted, as she had the first time he had done so.

"Dora deserves this, doesn't she?" Amelia sighed, moments later.

"If you say so, m'dear. But I must remind you I'm taken," Lord Lavenham responded with a crooked smile. He renewed his assault, and Amelia, heedless of the fixed stares of the servants—all pretending to look elsewhere, the lambs!—didn't think about her friend Dora for the rest of the evening.

CHAPTER SEVEN

LADY LAVENHAM'S PARTIES were always original. Last year, she informed her friend Dora when that lady paid another morning call in Portman Square, her grand ball had been the event of the season. The ballroom had become an Eastern seraglio for the evening, and the *Morning Post* had described it as a "glittering oasis of Oriental opulence." This year, it would follow its own Palladian architecture more closely, though no less dramatically, and would become a Roman forum. Dora, sworn to secrecy on the decoration— part of Amelia's tradition was deadly silence on that subject until the great moment arrived—pointed out, very unromantically, that people would not dance in a forum. And Amelia, tossing her head, merely informed her friend that not only would people dance in *her* forum, but this year she would have something new: ladies and gentlemen would be required to wear masks. Not fancy dress or dominoes, only masks with regular evening clothes.

"It sounds delightful," Dora returned. "But I must tell you now, dear, that I won't be able to attend."

Amelia stared.

"You see, Cousin Maud would never miss an event like this, so Augusta will already have a chaperone," Dora explained. She had been giving this matter a great deal of thought, and exciting though the Lavenham ball would undoubtedly be, she expected that for her it would be only a complicated evening of avoiding Sir James Perry and casting longing gazes from afar at Mr. Carruthers.

"Not that old tune again," Amelia sighed. "You know very well that I shall insist to Lady Bracken that you be included. I don't expect she'll refuse."

Dora had to admit that her story was getting rather old. Lady Bracken was almost enthusiastic about her companion's visits with the tonnish Lady Lavenham, and she already expected Theodora to attend the ball. Dora decided to be frank with her old friend. "I really don't think I could bear being pursued by Sir James and his giggling terrors of daughters for an entire evening," she admitted. "And he told me, when Augusta and I encountered him and his daughters in the park, that he had received your invitation. So I don't see how—"

"Nothing easier," said Amelia. "What do you think the masks are for, you silly creature? I'll simply misdirect Sir James when he arrives. I'm certain some other blonde ladies will be in attendance, and I'll send him off on the track of someone else while you enjoy yourself with quite another sort of cavalier."

Dora glanced sharply at Lady Lavenham's placid face. "Did you have a little matchmaking in mind, Amelia? I won't stand for it, you know."

"And no more you should," Amelia stated, patting Dora's hand. "I wouldn't in your place."

Dora still looked suspicious, but she made no further comments. It would seem that she was to attend this ball, whether she liked it or not.

THE LAVENHAM MANSION BLAZED with lights and noise on the happy night of Amelia's Roman affair. "Oh, Dora," whispered Augusta, her eyes shining through the slits in her white velvet mask, "how exciting. I never thought I'd attend a masked ball."

The two were climbing the main staircase of the Lavenham residence, in step behind Sir Giles and Lady Bracken. Dora, in her familiar blue ball gown and the matching mask, embroidered with violets, which she had made herself, was inclined to agree with her young cousin. If Sir James Perry could somehow be avoided, what a delightful evening this might be! The anonymity of the masks made everything seem lighthearted and easy.

Amelia was standing with Lord Lavenham, greeting each guest and making everyone tell their identity, though, in the spirit of the occasion, the butler was not announcing names. "Sir Giles, I would know you anywhere," she cried as the Bracken party approached her. "Wouldn't you, Freddy? It is that certain glint in this dear man's eyes, even through a mask. I always know he's laughing at me."

"Never, dear lady," protested Sir Giles, kissing his hostess's hand. "Well, Lavenham," he continued to his host, "your wife's got quite an eye. There's no hiding one's identity here."

"Quite. Amelia's a clever 'un," Lord Lavenham agreed noncommittally. "Bracken, is it? How d'ye do? We're getting up some whist tables before long. What say to that?"

Sir Giles's agreement to anything which would rescue him from the duties of the ballroom could usually be counted on to be swift and certain. He said he'd be glad to join Lord Lavenham as soon as he got his ladies settled.

"Dora," whispered Amelia, having first pressed her cheek to Lady Bracken's and given Augusta a friendly nod, "I've done it. Sent Sir James off after Cornelia Cummings. Don't I deserve special consideration for that?"

Dora laughed. "All I have to give is a compliment. You're looking very lovely, dear. And so... Roman!"

"Yes, aren't I?" Amelia, charmingly in tune with her fictional surroundings, had on a white dress trimmed in dark green velvet leaves, with a wreath of the same crowning her auburn curls. A green gauze shawl was draped about her in approximately the manner of a stola. "Now do go enjoy yourself. I'll join you later."

Dora, at the side of the fidgety Augusta, stepped down into the ballroom and laughed aloud. Amelia had indeed achieved an effect, but of what? It wasn't quite Roman, but it was enchanting and charming—like Amelia. A number of purple draperies had been brought into a ballroom that was white-columned to begin with; these draperies were edged in a Greek key pattern, the contradiction between this and a Roman forum obviously having escaped Lady Lavenham. And she seemed to have collected every classical vase and Roman-looking bust in London.

A wealth of laurel boughs framed the guests, an exotic group in evening dress set off by party masks. Dora noticed at once that her own homemade mask was absurdly simple; some, perhaps making up for the lack of an opportunity to dress in character, were wearing more elaborate headgear. Dora particularly admired one lady's hat which was in the shape of a swan, ending in a regular loo-mask covering the eyes. There were elephants, crocodiles and all sorts of birds made on this model, but on second glance Dora did see many other masks like hers, Lady Bracken's and Augusta's—simple satin or velvet ones made to match its wearer's gown. And most men had on plain black masks on the model of Sir Giles's. It was difficult to recognize people all the same. Dora frowned over the identity of a young gentleman who was approaching Augusta with a sense of purpose. Was that Lieutenant Flagg? Or the honourable Hugo Smythe-Wilton, another of Augusta's young admirers?

The young man got out a rather husky request to be allowed to conduct "the young lady" into the next set. Dora was certain his voice was disguised. Well, it was all in the spirit of fun. He was a rather tall young gentleman, with dark hair and a suit of clothes not quite in the mode.

Augusta made a hasty, rather nervous assent. But Lady Bracken, eyes snapping behind the crystal-encrusted cloth of gold confection that was vaguely reminiscent of some harsh Tudor queen, showed her displeasure. "Exactly who are you, young man? My daughter has many *eligible* gentlemen who are eager to see her tonight."

Sir Giles surveyed the youth with more mildness and said, "My dear, how can you demand someone's name at an affair of this sort? This lad looks harmless enough, and he and Augusta will be under your careful eye. Run along, my child." He gave Augusta a little push, leading Dora to suspect that Sir Giles knew, and approved of, the strange young man. Augusta's blue eyes, shadowed by the white mask, betrayed a very evident shock at her father's action, but she scampered off with her partner before Lady Bracken could get another word out.

"Well, Sir Giles!" she exclaimed in indignation. "How could you send our daughter off with that young sprout, when you know Captain Thomas Laughton and Mr. Carruthers are both longing to see her tonight?"

"They can see her better from out on the floor," Sir Giles said with a shrug. "Besides, Maud, for all you know that young gentleman she just went off with could be heir to a dukedom."

Lady Bracken gasped and fanned herself. "Sir Giles! Is he?" she asked eagerly.

"Not to my knowledge. But let the girl have her fun, m'dear. That's what we brought her to London for."

"You know we brought her to London to marry well," Lady Bracken retorted, to Sir Giles's and Dora's carefully hidden amusement, "and that is not the same thing." She settled herself in the classical-style hard chair which her husband held for her and patted its arm. "Amelia Lavenham must have borrowed these. I know for a fact her ballroom chairs are spindly little gilt-and-velvet things. She hasn't used them since the Versailles motif she did in the year of the Peace Celebrations. Well, that's nothing to the purpose. Do sit down, cousin Theodora. Sir Giles will find you another of these. Quite comfortable, I must admit. Now, my dear—" she turned to her husband, who was obediently settling Dora next to his wife and struggling to control his twitching lips "—do go away before you next give our daughter permission to dance with a bear. I'm out of patience with you."

Sir Giles lifted his lady's hand to his lips. "But my love! Am I to take it you won't favour me with this dance?"

Lady Bracken was suddenly all coy simpers and batting eyes. "Why, but I must watch Augusta, and you never dance, Sir Giles."

"My loss, I'm sure. Cousin Theodora will watch the young people, won't you, Cousin?" At Dora's dazed nod—for she had never heard of the Brackens dancing together, and suspected Sir Giles was trying to draw his lady's attention away from her daughter for some unfathomable reason—he clasped his wife's arm and went off with her to join a set that was, Dora noticed, far distant from the place where Augusta and her incognito were standing.

Dora, mindful of her duty, fastened her eyes on the young pair. They seemed to know each other, from the amount of chattering Augusta was doing and the way the young gentleman was bending his head down to hers to talk back with quite as much freedom. Well, Augusta knew several gentlemen—one really ought to say boys—who fit the general description of her masked partner, and there was no mystery about it. Augusta rattled on to gentlemen with much more ease than Dora ever had at that age, or even now, in her advanced years, she mused. As her eyes strayed from the young pair, she began to enjoy in a more general way the colourful pageant taking place around her.

She leaned back in the ebony chair, little aware of how charming a picture she made in her simple silk gown, the ribbons of her mask disarranging her hair a little from its knot of curls in an almost wanton, and very flattering manner. She did wish that she were not quite so open a target for Sir James Perry, who would certainly not be taken in by Amelia's ruse for long and would hunt her down. After this tune was over, Dora planned to excuse herself to Lady Bracken, saying she had to repair a hem, and watch the next dances from some private alcove. She knew Amelia's ballroom must be full of such places. Even a chair behind one of the laurel boughs would be some cover.

Realizing that she was thinking exactly as a fox might, Dora let out a laugh. And no sooner had she done so than a very tall, dark gentleman with compelling hazel eyes visible through a black silk mask was bowing before her.

It was he! It was definitely Mr. Carruthers. Dora beamed up at the man, amazed at her luck. She didn't greet him, for Amelia had been very strict about at least the appearance of anonymity being maintained until midnight.

"Fair lady." It was Carruthers's voice. "How glad I am to see you. Our hostess said I might find you here. They are playing a waltz next. May I hope to have the pleasure?"

"Why..." Dora hesitated. That Amelia! Matchmaking whether her victims wished it or no. "I can hardly disappear before the rest of my party comes back, but yes, sir, I would love to waltz. Am I correct in assuming that we're acquainted?''

"No one is acquainted at a masked ball, dear madam. But we have waltzed before.'' Carruthers sat down in the chair Lady Bracken had briefly occupied and prepared to wait out the quadrille in progress.

Before long both Augusta and her parents were bearing down on them. Augusta, Dora noticed, was alone. Her young mystery partner had chosen not to take a second dose of Lady Bracken's abrasiveness, then. That lady, bright and glowing in the wake of a dance with her husband, positively sparkled when she saw who was sitting with Dora. The gentleman rose and made her, and Augusta, who was next to her, his best bow.

"Why, Mr.—Oh, I forget, we mustn't use names here. How very glad we all are to see you. I'm certain my daughter's next dance is free. She's just been allowed the waltz, you know. Madame de Lieven gave her permission only last Wednesday. Go on, my sweet. Mama will be watching to see you don't miss a step.''

"You mistake, ma'am,'' Carruthers broke in with a smile. "I was waiting to greet your party before taking *this* charming lady out to dance.''

"Oh.'' Lady Bracken's tone changed instantly, and her eyes swept over Dora. "I'm so sorry, sir, but you don't quite understand Miss, er, this lady's position with us. She is my companion, you know.'' She paused dramatically.

The gentleman didn't draw back in horror, as Lady Bracken might have counted on. He merely replied, "I know her position with you, ma'am, but in this house she is a guest of the Lavenhams', and as such, entitled to dance, wouldn't you say?''

Dora remained silent out of pure embarrassment.

The debate went on. "But my cousin and companion—paid companion, I might add—is also under my protection, sir. And I don't think it would be quite seemly if she were to take the floor. I wasn't present at the other ball she attended, or I certainly would have put a stop to it. In her situation...you understand." Lady Bracken smiled as sweetly as she could.

"Mama, you're being ridiculous," Augusta put in, catching at her mother's sleeve.

"Miss, you forget yourself," her mother hissed. "I'll put it to our cousin. Theodora, you don't wish to dance, do you? I know how concerned you are at all times with decorum."

Dora, whose face had been reddening with rage behind the innocent violet-trimmed mask, wished she had the courage to snap back at her cousin Maud that she hadn't been proposing to dance naked! But she couldn't say such a thing in mixed company, so she merely responded, "I saw no harm in it, but if your ladyship would be displeased, I'm certain I can better spend the time talking to my hostess. She—and someone who looks very like Lady Jersey, whom I see sitting with her right now—will be able to direct my manners if anyone else should ask me to dance this evening." She stood up. "Excuse me."

Mr. Carruthers caught at her arm. "Ma'am, I'm going to insist over your objections—as I did last time we danced, by the way, Lady Bracken. Shall we? And Miss Bracken, if you'll save me the boulanger later this evening?"

Lady Bracken opened her mouth and closed it again. A rebuke to oneself and a compliment to one's daughter uttered within seconds of one another! What was the proper response?

"I'd be delighted, sir," Augusta agreed with a very demure look. "How naughty of you. You forgot Lady

Lavenham didn't want names used. Do go on now, both of you. I'll take care of Mama.''

Her elbow firmly clasped in the strong hand of Mr. Carruthers, Dora moved out among the dancers. The lilting strains of a Steibelt waltz were just beginning. Carruthers's arm encircled her waist; his large hand caressed the area just above the curve of her hip. Dora knew she should tell him to behave himself, but she simply couldn't. She would enjoy his touch. For once in her life she wouldn't think of the proprieties.

"A penny for your thoughts?" Carruthers enquired.

Dora laughed. "I was only just now telling myself not to have any of those for the next little while."

"Charming. I'll follow your example and lose myself in your company. Are we agreed, then?" Mr. Carruthers's eyes were glittering. Dora lowered her own, suddenly grateful for the mask which concealed her confusion—at least that which her face betrayed. Her heart, though—surely he must hear it?

"I do enjoy dancing with you, sir," she said in a low voice. He had to bend his head down to hear the remark, but hear it he did. His smile broadened, and he swept her about the room holding her much more tightly to him than was proper. Dora didn't protest; she was enjoying the sensation too much. The music ended to their mutual chagrin, and Carruthers returned the lady to her glaring chaperone, made a charming bow and ambled down the room, a look of bemusement on his face.

FROM BENEATH a bird-of-paradise headdress, a pair of dark, paint-rimmed eyes had been watching these manoeuvres with suspicion. Before Carruthers had made a full circle about the Roman forum, a slim, gloved hand reached out and captured his arm. "Monsieur," said an all-too-familiar voice, "a word."

"My God!" Carruthers stared. "How the devil? The Lavenhams didn't invite you, surely?"

"You insult, as always, but I forgive," the vision before him said with a shrug and a pout. Dark, shining hair, a lush figure, half-encased in a gown of jade-green silk, a frivolous bird mask with a gilded eye-piece, and the emeralds Carruthers had given her for her last birthday. It was Yvette, beyond a doubt. "May we be more private?" she added plaintively, gesturing to the crowds surrounding them.

"With pleasure, my dear." And, walking ahead of his ex-mistress in a way that made her seethe—for why should he be ashamed of her, forsooth? she was the best-looking woman in the room—Carruthers led the way to a secluded antechamber that opened into the ballroom. There were several of these, and he had the luck to hit on an unoccupied one—no great trick, as the hour was still early. Couples who would dally later would still be furthering their acquaintance in the dance.

Carruthers closed the door. "Now," he said in crisp tones, "what is the meaning of this?"

Yvette removed her mask, ran her hands over her hair, and faced her former protector. "Why, I have friends. You would be surprised at the places I may go if I wish, Laurent."

The French inflection she gave his name had once aroused amorous thoughts in Carruthers; now, it irritated him. "You've had the audacity to show up at the Lavenhams' ball, I can see that. And I imagine that any number of bucks will be bragging tomorrow that you graced this gathering through their ingenuity. But might I ask why? I don't dare think you might still be interested in my affairs."

Yvette sank down on a delicate white sofa, the only piece of furniture in the little room. "Not only interested, *chéri*, but also confused. I see you with the lady in blue—ah, there is the bride, I tell myself. Then I ask the questions, and I find that she is only a paid companion—a *suivante*. A poor relation, *enfin*, and not even young. It is another person, a child in white, whom the gossips link you with. The young lady's *maman*, she is very certain of the outcome, it would seem."

Carruthers burst out laughing. "Good Lord, Yvette, is that what you've heard?"

"*Oui*. And I must ask you—for my curiosity only, you comprehend—which is it to be?"

Carruthers caught the note of calculation in the voice of his former ladybird, and he suspected that mere curiosity was not her whole motive.

"As a woman, you understand, I am naturally *curieuse*. Who has won out over Yvette?" the lounging female continued smoothly.

Carruthers eyed her with disapprobation tempered by a little pity. The world was not a pretty place for Yvette's sort, and he suspected that she was beginning to learn that for the first time. He had nothing to say to her, really; he would certainly not help her to an exact knowledge of the woman he was pursuing. He was certain that Yvette wouldn't dare approach any woman of good reputation, but she might find a way to do mischief if she knew too much. However, he felt he owed her an answer of sorts. "My dear, you are without an equal," he said, reasoning that it was the truth. Then he bowed and left the room, certain that Yvette would not need to be reminded to leave the party before the unmasking hour.

Inside the little sanctuary, Yvette was already putting her mask back on. Her lovely face was set in determination. She

knew dear Laurent very well. He thought he had told her
nothing, the fool. Pah! Men were such children.

IN ANOTHER PART of the ballroom, Dora was having prob-
lems of her own. The hour of twelve had just struck, and the
guests, with much laughter and good-natured joking, removed their masks to reveal faces flushed with dancing,
wine and the late hour. Dora took off her mask and placed
it in her reticule. Augusta, she must suppose, was doing the
same thing across the floor in the company of her current
partner, young Mr. Graham. Lady Bracken, silently sitting
beside Dora—the ladies had been pointedly avoiding exces-
sive speech with one another—removed her elegant confection of gold and sparkling beads.

Captain Thomas Laughton happened to be standing beside the two women. He had just finished a dance with
Dora, to Lady Bracken's dismay. He had been wearing a
headdress in the shape of a dragon; something a friend had
sent him from China, he had confided. "Well, ladies, now
that I've seen your faces in all their loveliness, I must leave
you. My sister is counting on me to take her and the general
in to supper, more's the pity. She has told me in no uncertain terms not to strand her with our uncle, though I'd much
rather stay with you." And his fine blue eyes rested an instant longer on Dora than on Lady Bracken.

"My *daughter* will be disappointed, Captain, but we must
excuse you. Give our best to Lady Vining. And the dear
general," Lady Bracken answered in a haughty manner. She
was not best pleased with this gentleman's behaviour. Why,
the swine had not even asked Augusta to dance! And now
he was off to play nursemaid to his bosky old reprobate of
an uncle before Augusta even returned! Of course, the dear
child had been constantly on the floor ever since the captain had found their party, and he hadn't really had a chance

to dance with her. Yes, that must be it. It couldn't be that this eligible gentleman had a real interest in Cousin Theodora, any more than Mr. Carruthers did. They were only being excessively polite to a cousin of Augusta's.

The captain made a graceful bow and moved away. In the next moment two young girls ran shrieking up to the ladies. "Miss Thornfield!" they chorused. "We knew you weren't the lady in yellow sarcenet. We knew it all the time."

Dora gave a weak smile. Miss Perry and Miss Alice, Sir James Perry's two daughters, giggled in delight.

"I'll fetch Papa," cried Miss Alice, a tall, gangling girl. She loped off.

Lady Bracken smiled kindly on her cousin for the first time since Dora's unfortunate dance with Lawrence Carruthers. "How sweet. The dear girls have been seeking you out for their father. Such a solid, respectable man. I must tell you, Caroline—" she turned toward Miss Perry, who stood by with the air of a hunting dog who has treed its prey "—I mean to encourage this little romance."

Dora groaned. Caroline leered.

"Papa talks of nothing but Miss Thornfield," the girl said helpfully.

Alice soon reappeared, her father in tow. Dora's middle-aged suitor was puffing slightly in the wake of his daughter's quick pace. "Miss Thornfield!" he said in a hearty voice. "And dear Lady Bracken. Ah, ladies, ladies. These masked parties are sad things. Here I've spent two hours at least thinking our dear Miss Thornfield was quite another lady. But now that I've found you, ma'am, may I prevail upon you to take supper with my daughters and me?"

"Oh, do," the girls chimed.

"I ought to sit with my cousins," Dora said weakly, knowing that there would be no escape.

"Heavens, Cousin Theodora, go on with this dear man and his sweet daughters. It isn't as though I have need of you," Lady Bracken put in, as Dora had known she would.

The movement to the supper room was beginning, and Sir James, flushed with victory, offered Dora his arm. His daughters giggled, saying that they would go find their aunt and then join Papa and his charming partner. They would have such a comfortable coze, all getting to know one another better.

Dora shuddered as she walked off under the triumphant eye of Lady Bracken. Sir James began an anecdote involving his two youngest boys, who were giving their nurse such trouble. "They are lively boys, you understand," he told his captive listener. "Their two baby sisters are as yet unable to join in their pranks—did you know my late wife was carried off giving birth to twins, dear Miss Thornfield?—and they see their four older brothers so rarely, all those boys being at school. Then there is my married daughter Cynthia, but she lives such a way off. In Shropshire. They have a charming manor in a very rustic, secluded area, which my whole family delights in visiting. Ah, but it is difficult, dear Miss Thornfield, for my children to obtain the kind of guidance which is most necessary at their varied times in life. A mother's care, Miss Thornfield. Ah, what can equal a mother's care?"

Dora had been making mental calculations, and had come up with the alarming figure of eleven. Lady Perry had given her life in the dubious cause of augmenting this boring gentleman's family, and now a new sacrifice, a simple spinster who would presumably be grateful for marriage at any price, was to be set upon the pyre. No. Dora set her jaw in determination. She wouldn't even thank Sir James for the flowers. Oh, if only nice Captain Laughton hadn't had to leave after his one dance with her.

Then she forgot Captain Laughton's existence, for she caught sight of Mr. Carruthers. He was standing near the front door, which the guests bound for supper had to pass on their way to the lower rooms where the meal was laid out. He had on his hat, worse luck. And he was deep in conversation with someone, a young man with dark hair and a serious, earnest face.

Dora looked harder. It was one of Augusta's partners, the masked young stranger whom Lady Bracken had taken such exception to, and whom Sir Giles had seemed to approve. So, he knew Carruthers.

There was nothing extraordinary in two guests at the same party being acquainted with one another. But that young man still had the look of mystery about him, even without the mask, and Dora couldn't help wondering who he was. Sir Giles had seemed to know him; Carruthers had a speaking acquaintance with him; and he had danced with Augusta. Despite his rather inelegant dress, he must be someone of note.

CHAPTER EIGHT

THE NEXT AFTERNOON, at five, Augusta begged, with some urgency, that Dora walk out to the Park with her. "Mama is still resting after the party," she wheedled, "and she's given her permission. Do say you will, Cousin. I'm so longing to get out into the air."

"You are?" asked Dora in genuine astonishment. Augusta's indifference to such things as air and exercise almost equalled her mother's.

"Of course," insisted Augusta, steering Dora toward their bedchambers so that they could make ready for the outing. "Your lectures have finally paid off, Dora. I mean to turn over a new leaf and be quite healthy. And it's such a lovely, cool day."

Augusta did keep up a brisk, energetic pace all during the walk to Hyde Park, which, combined with the young girl's insistence on wearing her best and newest bonnet, roused Dora's suspicions. "My dear, you aren't making use of me to have an assignation with a young man, are you?" she asked as they entered the Park by the Stanhope Gate.

Eyes round with surprise, Augusta denied any such bold plan. "But naturally we'll meet gentlemen here. This is the Park, after all, Dora," she said to qualify her denial.

"Well, you're right about that," Dora had to concede. "It is indeed the Park. And let us hope that those gentlemen do not include Sir James Perry."

The cousins laughed together, for Dora had long since confided in Augusta her distaste of Sir James's suit, and the young girl, unlike Lady Bracken, had had no trouble understanding the reasons behind such an aversion.

They had not been strolling the path more than five minutes before a gentleman mounted on a fine white horse clattered toward them and came to a flourishing halt mere inches from where they stood at the edge of a crowd of promenaders, many of whom cast peeved glances at the bit of equestrian showmanship. "Captain Laughton!" cried both Augusta and Dora in pleasure.

"Ladies, I am charmed," the captain answered. He swung down from his mount to walk beside the ladies for a little distance.

"Miss Thornfield," said Laughton, giving Dora an intimate glance that confused her a little, "does this venture of yours mean that we'll be seeing you out more often? The Park is such a desert, we jaded Londoners are in need of a fresh new face."

"My face can hardly qualify," retorted Dora in the same joking spirit. "And I somehow can't see you, Captain, as a jaded Londoner."

"Well, can you see me as a pleasant companion for a walk, then?"

Both ladies assured Captain Laughton that he was much more than that, and they strolled along, bantering in a desultory fashion, possibly to the great annoyance of Laughton's spirited horse, pressed into service as an escort to ladies for the first time in his equine life. Then all at once Dora felt Augusta, whose arm was linked through hers, begin to quiver.

"My dear! What's the matter? Are you feeling ill?" Dora asked, eyeing the girl's pale face in concern. While she watched, Augusta's cheeks turned quite red.

"Oh!" said the young girl in an excited voice. "There is Mr. Carruthers."

Dora's heart sank. So Augusta was affected to this degree by the mere sight of that gentleman! How sad for the young girl, if Carruthers should be only trifling with her. Resisting her own slight tendency to tremble, Dora finally glanced in the direction Augusta had indicated.

There he was indeed, walking along the path toward them. Dora had to let out an involuntary sigh as her eyes lingered on Carruthers's tall, commanding figure, his raven hair glinting in the thin, spring sun, his handsome profile. Irritated, she realized that Augusta was sighing, too. Rather guiltily, Dora glanced out of the corner of her eye at Captain Laughton. She had completely forgotten about him. Though he was quite as handsome as Carruthers—in a different way, given his blond hair and slighter physique—no similar thrill had gone through Dora on first sight of him. What was wrong with her? According to all reports, the captain was much more accessible as a match for a penniless spinster than was that daunting bachelor, Carruthers.

That gentleman had seen the group, and he now came forward through the crowd. "Well met, Miss Bracken," he cried. "I believe my young companion here is an old friend of yours."

For the first time Dora noticed that there was a young man trailing slightly behind Carruthers—the same young man whom Augusta had danced with the night before!

Augusta's skin changed colour again, and Dora gave the young lady a sharp glance.

"Miss Thornfield, Captain Laughton—" Carruthers drew the young man forward for proper introductions "—may I present my heir, Mr. Edgar Farley. He is my second cousin, as it happens. He and his sister, Selina, and their mother are making a short visit to London."

Dora stared. Mr. Farley in London! No wonder Augusta was trembling and quaking and casting Dora such guilty looks. She had insisted on coming to the Park because she knew Mr. Farley would be here. She must be in love with him still to be acting so deceptive!

"We're staying with Cousin Carruthers," said Farley. He and Augusta were now smiling at each other with youthful shyness. "How are you, Augusta. Oh—" remembering his manners "—how do you do, Miss Thornfield, Captain Laughton."

Dora was mystified as to why Carruthers had invited Augusta's secret love to London. As far as anyone knew, the gentleman hadn't bothered with his Surrey connections at all in the past. Why the sudden reform to a close, cousinly relationship?

"You were at Lady Lavenham's ball last night, Mr. Farley," Dora said, endeavouring to cover up her surprise at the young man's identity.

Mr. Farley looked confused. "Well...yes. And I couldn't resist dancing once with Miss Bracken, to see if she'd recognize an old friend from the country."

"And did she?"

Augusta broke in. She had quite recovered her complexion and her natural manner. "Certainly, for Edgar is like a brother to me, you know, Dora. We've been so close for so many years."

Edgar Farley's young face dropped visibly at these words; and Dora, observing the way Augusta's eyes slid to Carruthers, did think it rather cruel that her young cousin should take such a public way of assuring the older man she was heart-free, at the expense of a boy she had only weeks ago proclaimed to be her only love.

Well, young things could be cruel, but their recovery time from ailments of the heart was also rather quick. Dora, after pausing to assure herself that whatever Carruthers's manner toward Augusta it was not that of a besotted admirer, devoted herself to poor Mr. Farley. The young man's real reaction to Augusta's comment could only be guessed, but he regained his pleasant expression quickly enough. Dora and Captain Laughton, whose sensitive blue eyes had also glimpsed an intrigue of some sort between the young man and Miss Bracken—and not a happy one—kept Mr. Farley busy answering questions while Augusta and Mr. Carruthers walked along on either side of the trio, maintaining a studied silence.

"Young man, you might find it very useful for your career, this visit to town," Captain Laughton said. "You say you've just been ordained? Well, there might be many gentlemen in town for the season who have livings in their gift. I have none, worse luck, but your cousin here is bound to introduce you to less useless landowners than I as time goes by."

"Er, yes," said Mr. Farley nervously, with a glance at Carruthers.

"I'll certainly see to it that my cousin makes use of his time in town," Mr. Carruthers put in, with a charming smile directed at Dora of all people.

"Capital," said Laughton with a nod, while Dora added her approval with a little curve of her lips. She had felt herself begin to blush, and this annoyed her.

"And now, with your future assured, Mr. Farley," the captain went on, "what of your present? Is this your first visit to town?"

Reawakened to animation, young Mr. Farley raved about the ball the night before—his first affair of that sort—and gave equal enthusiasm to his description of another excursion he had made since coming to town the other day: to see the Elgin marbles. When he found that none of the others save Carruthers had seen them, the young man grew even more eloquent.

"I have a feeling it made my poor sister tired to hang about so long with me," he finished with a shy smile. "But I've dreamed for years of seeing the marbles."

Dora reflected that a young man so serious about classical artefacts was not at all the sort of person to hold Augusta's affection. What a shame, for Mr. Farley was still gazing at the young girl with every appearance of attachment, though Augusta had so crudely set him down into the role of brother, and was not looking at him at all.

"Talking of sight-seeing trips," Mr. Carruthers said taking up the conversation, "one reason I'm glad to meet with you today, Miss Thornfield—and Miss Bracken—is to invite you to come down and view my country place in Buckinghamshire. It's about an hours' drive from here, and I'm taking my cousins out next week, only for the day, you know, to see the park and so on. Mrs. Farley used to visit the estate in my father's time, and her children have never seen it. What do you think, Miss Bracken? Would your mother like such a trip? It's set for Thursday, but we could alter that to suit her ladyship's convenience."

"Oh! You mean to take Mama." Augusta's crestfallen look was not supremely flattering to Lady Bracken, and the other members of the group struggled to maintain their seriousness. "I'm sure she'd like it above all things," she was forced to concede. "And we have no plans yet for Thursday."

Laughton had been standing by, looking expectant. Finally Carruthers noticed him and perforce invited him along, too, "if you'd not be bored with a simple country outing of this sort," he added.

The captain said slyly, "How could any gathering which includes Miss Thornfield be boring?"

"Oh, but I shan't be going," Dora protested. "I'm certain Lady Bracken won't require me."

"But the rest of us will," Carruthers assured her, looking directly into her eyes with a keen expression. "We won't argue the point here, ma'am, but be warned that your modesty and unwillingness to join in amusements as you should will not stand against the combined efforts of myself, our charming Miss Bracken and, er, Captain Laughton."

"Sir!" said Dora with a blush, and the gentleman responded by raising her hand to his lips and kissing it, under the romantically jealous eye of Captain Laughton. Though she was embarrassed, this was the brightest moment of Dora's day.

None of the party happened to notice the elegant tilbury which at that instant was passing near them on the carriage road. Nor did they see the vehicle's occupant, a beautiful, dark-haired lady dressed fashionably in deep rose velvet, survey the little group with a very definite look of malice.

DORA AND HER CHARGE were mounting the steps of the Bracken house by the time the elder cousin was able to ask casually, "Well, my dear, you must be very pleased to see your Mr. Farley in town. I know how much you've missed him."

Augusta's little face assumed a closed, furtive expression. "Missed him? Oh! Yes, of course I was homesick for everything in Surrey when we first came to town. How silly we are when we are young."

With this one flippant comment Mr. Farley was dismissed. Dora, distressed for the young man, whom she could swear still admired Augusta, decided that the expected had happened, and Augusta was now languishing after someone else. And who of the men the young girl knew was more appealing, more romantic, than Lawrence Carruthers?

The two went right up to see Augusta's mama, who had been forced to spend the day in her boudoir after the exertion of the ball. Lady Bracken was ecstatic when she heard that Lawrence Carruthers was organizing a country fête at his Buckinghamshire estate. "Ashvale is quite the showplace," she proclaimed, casting glance after knowing glance at her daughter. "I'm certain he has a particular interest in your seeing his home, dear child. And you're absolutely correct, Cousin Theodora, I shan't require you on that day. You may stay here and catch up on your letters, or whatever it is you do by yourself."

Dora set her teeth, the more chagrined since this was a pretty accurate description of her idle hours.

"But Mama," Augusta chimed in, "Mr. Carruthers said most particularly that he wanted Dora to come."

"He did!" Lady Bracken stared. Then, recollecting herself, she continued, "Well, what else could he have said, with her standing right there? You really shouldn't angle for invitations, Cousin. It isn't becoming. And Mr. Carruthers will certainly understand your begging off with a headache. Don't worry. I shall handle everything."

Dora, very near to snapping Cousin Maud's head off, adhered to the new system she had devised for such occasions. She peremptorily excused herself to go to her room and take off her bonnet.

"And a very showy bonnet it is for someone of her station," Lady Bracken snapped as soon as the door had closed behind her. "I can't think where the creature got such clothes, with her lack of funds. Her sisters' charity, no doubt."

"Mama!" protested Augusta.

Lady Bracken remembered belatedly that Cousin Theodora and her daughter were great friends. "Oh, you know Mama can be cattish when she's tired, darling. Now tell me more about this trip into Buckinghamshire. Will Mr. Carruthers require me to be his hostess? Sad man, he really should marry—but we'll say no more on that score for the moment."

"Well, Mama, I believe a relation of his is going, an older lady," Augusta said in answer to her mother's question.

"An older lady? Hmm, I wonder if she is anyone we know," mused Lady Bracken, leaning back on her couch. "It can't be his aunt, old Violet Osmore, for she hasn't stirred from Bath in decades. Augusta, do bring a pillow from the window seat for Mama's back. That cousin of ours is never around when I need her. I don't know why I put up with—Ah, thank you, my dear."

Augusta did not say a word as she attended to her mama's comfort with much more energy than she usually brought to the task. Somehow, in the bustle of settling pillows and pouring out a cordial and ringing for the dresser—for it was getting near to dinnertime—the question of Mr. Carruthers's hostess was forgotten.

CHAPTER NINE

As soon as she was able, Dora cornered Sir Giles and asked him bluntly if he had known that Mr. Farley had attended the Lavenham ball. This fortuitous opportunity occurred when Dora happened to be walking out on an errand for Lady Bracken at her usual time for such tasks, the same early hour Sir Giles commonly left for his club. After a brief consultation, they had elected to walk down Albemarle Street together.

Sir Giles shrugged and smiled his sardonic smile. "Why, how could I not recognize him, my dear? I've known the boy for years."

"Then you did know it was Mr. Farley whom Augusta was dancing with," Dora exclaimed. "You even seemed to approve it. But why, sir? I was under the impression—that is, your daughter told me some time ago that you and Cousin Maud didn't approve her attachment to the young man."

Winking, Sir Giles answered, "I think the lad would be a fine match for my silly little daughter. Seems to settle her down to be with him. He wasn't ordained for no reason— he's a serious sort of fellow. It's Maud that looks for greater things than a country clergyman. And I wasn't forthcoming when the young people first wanted to marry, not only because Augusta was too young, but because young Farley had no prospects. I hadn't a living to give him. But now, with him in London, who knows what might happen? My friend Carruthers has influence, and the lad's his heir. Didn't know that before, either."

Dora nodded, digesting this.

"But," Sir Giles continued, with another insouciant shrug, "who's to say now? Could be the girl's head's been turned by her visit to town. Farley might want her now, but the question is, does she want Farley?"

"Poor Mr. Farley." Dora sighed. "Yesterday she said, right in front of him, that he was like a brother to her. I'm afraid you're right about Augusta's feelings, sir. Whoever it is she wants now, I'm afraid it isn't her old admirer."

"Time will tell," Sir Giles said cheerfully. "Wouldn't it fox Maudie, though? Bring the girl all the way to town, rig her out at ruinous expense and marry her off in the end to her old beau from Surrey." He chuckled wickedly.

Dora, though she forebore to join him in this unkind re-action to Lady Bracken's certain dismay, did wish Sir Giles's fantasy might come to pass. For purely altruistic reasons, she told herself. It would be a shame to see Mr. Farley hurt.

Dora bade Sir Giles good day, watched him cross Picadilly en route to St. James' Street, and herself turned the corner into Old Bond, making for a certain shop which held precisely the colour of ribbon Lady Bracken needed to match the trimming on a gown. Rummaging through her reticule as she walked along—yes, she had brought the scrap of satin with her—Dora was still sighing over poor Mr. Farley's fate. So intent was she on her thoughts that she didn't see the lady until she had almost trodden on her fine kid half boots.

"Oh! Pardon me, ma'am," Dora murmured automatically, sketching a vague curtsey. She tried to pass.

"*Mademoiselle*, if I might beg a moment of your time?" a rich, prettily accented voice asked.

Dora looked up and beheld, facing her on the pavement, a beautiful dark-haired woman of indeterminate years, clad in a costly pelisse of cherry-red velvet trimmed with swansdown, and an obviously Parisian bonnet rakishly ornamented with a sweeping plume and a bunch of cherries. Somehow, Dora felt her own pelisse of drab broadcloth had been reduced on the spot to the merest rag.

"Do we know each other, *madame*?" Dora asked curiously, though she was certain she would have remembered meeting such a striking person.

"Not yet," the other lady admitted with a smile. "But we are connected in a way. You come with me now, *n'est-ce pas?* My carriage is right here, and it is more private, *oui*?"

Dora's eyes turned to the road. There was a gold-wheeled barouche, drawn by a pair of blue-black horses. The door of the vehicle was emblazoned with a cockade that matched the one in the jaunty hat of the driver, who was dressed in ornate red-and-purple livery. Despite the look of prosperity, there was the hint of something strange, something sinister, about the whole equipage. For heaven's sake, did brothel-keepers prey on middle-aged spinsters? Surely not. "Drive with you, ma'am? But as I'm persuaded we are strangers..."

"Ah, we might not be acquainted, Mademoiselle Thornfield, but there is a friend of both of ours, a Monsieur Carruthers—" the unknown woman said the name oddly, but Dora understood it "—and it is of that friend that you and I must—how you say?—have speech."

Yvette had been in England for nigh on thirty years and spoke the language to perfection, but she still found the occasional affectation of recent *emigrée* worked to her advantage.

Dora's eyes had widened at the mention of Carruthers's name. "You are a friend of his, ma'am? And wish to talk of him? In what connection, might I ask?"

Yvette glanced furtively about the street. Passersby were indeed examining the two women with interest, though likely as yet no permanent damage had been done. They were on a shopping street, and it was early in the day. Hardly any people of fashion were out and about, and most of those were women, who would never have seen Yvette off the stage and would not be likely to identify her. Still, it would be safer to be away.

"All will become clear to you, *mademoiselle*, if you will but accompany me. It will not take long, you understand. It is but a step to the house in Charles Street. *Mademoiselle*—I beg of you." Yvette's years upon the stage came to her aid as she coaxed tears from her wonderful dark eyes. "He...he will hear of it if we stand here much longer, and I need so badly to talk with you. Oh, *mademoiselle*, he will be so angry." She burst out crying, making use of a lace handkerchief and all the dramatic talent she possessed. "I do so long to speak to you. There is so much I must tell you. Ah, it is such a small thing, a short carriage ride, a few moments..."

Dora was quite taken in by this show of distress. Whatever this mystery about Carruthers was, the lady was obviously in need of solace. "I will go with you to Charles Street," Dora decided on the spot, casting nervous glances about her. The woman was right; they were already under observation. "Please calm yourself, ma'am. Everything will be all right." It was broad daylight, and surely no harm could come to one, driving a short distance along these streets. Why, if the lady turned out to be a cutpurse, Dora might safely enough jump down from her vehicle. Besides—and this was what clinched Dora's decision to go with the woman—Cousin Maud would have the vapours if she could see her companion mounting such a dubious vehicle, for a ride to a strange lady's house.

Yvette smiled through her tears, dabbing at her eyes. A footman jumped down from the barouche and handed both women inside.

"What is this about Mr. Carruthers?" Dora asked as soon as the coach was moving. "Why is he being so harsh with you? Is he a close friend of yours?" As she looked at her richly dressed hostess, the suspicions that had plagued Dora at the foreign lady's first mention of Carruthers returned with a renewed force. It couldn't be . . . but who else *would* it be? She had to find out.

No answer to her question was forthcoming. The lady remained silent except for the occasional sniffle—she was still in tears. Finally Dora continued, with a shaky smile, "You have the advantage of me, ma'am. You know my name, yet I have not the same pleasure."

"Have patience, *mademoiselle*," murmured the other, leaning back upon the satin squabs of her chariot. She was still crying softly to all appearances, but she had calmed down.

Dora shrugged and lapsed into silence, looking out on the passing scene as the carriage bowled along the streets of Mayfair. Soon they were halting before a black-painted door in Charles Street, a door identical to a score of others. The two ladies were handed down.

"Do come in, *ma chère*," Yvette invited, motioning for her quarry to mount the steps in front of her. She rang, explaining in an aside, "I never have my key," and a starchy-looking butler answered the door. "We will be in the rose salon, Farnham," Yvette announced, sailing in. "Bring . . . tea, I think, and brandy. *Oui*, we may have need of brandy."

Mystified, Dora followed, wondering in a detached sort of way whether she was about to be clubbed over the head and held for ransom in this pleasant, rich-looking house. Who did they think would pay for her safety? Mr. Carruthers?

But it was not kidnapping that awaited Dora that day; rather it was an upset of quite another sort. Her hostess led the way into a drawing room and closed the door behind them both. Dora looked about her.

It was a common-enough sort of room. The furnishings were too overblown for Dora's taste; she had never found the rococo to be pleasing, but she knew that many members of the ton did have salons that featured satin settees and plush chairs wrought heavily in gold. Over the mantel was a portrait of a female in a reclining position. Dora blushed and looked away. The lady in the painting was totally unclothed. Then Dora had to look back to study the face, for a resemblance had struck her. Yes, it was her hostess!

"Sit down, I pray you, *mademoiselle*," Yvette invited. Having taken off the red pelisse to reveal a low-cut gown of pristine white, she followed her own advice, coming to rest upon a pink-and-gold striped chaise longue.

Dora, reticule clutched tightly in her hands and pelisse buttoned up to the neck, took a chair opposite. The woman's earlier mention of Carruthers, and the presence of such a shocking portrait, had finally made Dora certain enough to voice what must be the truth. "Pardon, ma'am, but would your name possibly be Yvette?"

The other lady smiled. "You have heard of me?"

"Well, very indirectly." Dora looked earnestly into the woman's face. This was a Cyprian! She, Theodora Thornfield, veteran of many an hour spent serving soup to the cottagers of Thorne Park, not to mention a surfeit of time in the nurseries of her sisters' genteel houses, was face-to-face with a woman of easy virtue!

Yvette shrugged. "I would not expect him to have mentioned me. Laurent, he is not one to go into particulars."

Dora gaped. "Laurent?"

"Carruthers," Yvette clarified. "We have, naturally, spoken of you." She ignored her guest's shocked intake of breath. "Tell me, *ma chère*, does the house please you?"

Ignoring that question, Dora cried, "You and Mr. Carruthers have spoken of me? Of *me*?"

"But yes. Many times." Yvette's voice was light, casual. "It is our way, you know. Ah, but you are new at this trade, *n'est-ce pas*? Perhaps you did not realize."

"Realize what?" Dora got out in a squeaky little voice she barely recognized as her own.

"That gentlemen are of the habit to discuss with their mistresses the question of the...successor." In a pleasant offhand voice, Yvette completely finished Dora's self-possession.

"Oh, my Lord, you can't mean it," she managed to croak out before she got to her feet, shaky though they were, and stalked to the door. As she arrived there it opened to disclose the butler, armed with a tray of tea, brandy and various oddments.

Yvette suddenly began to bustle about, directing Farnham where to place the tray and insisting he take Miss Thornfield's things, which Dora as firmly refused to surrender.

"I am leaving now, ma'am." She bit out the words.

Yvette, reverting to the tactics that had worked the best, squeezed out some more tears and flung herself upon the chaise, face-down. The butler prudently withdrew.

Dora softened immediately and approached the Cyprian. It was very odd, but she felt almost the same undefinable guilt she suffered whenever she brought her sister Mary to tears. "Please, Miss Yvette, why do you keep crying? What is wrong?"

Yvette glanced up, eyes bright, face flushed. "It is simply this. You are to be the next inhabitant of this house, *mademoiselle*, his next lover. And I adore him! I simply must be assured that you will be worthy of him. Swear to me that you will take care of him, *mademoiselle*, that you will not leave him. For though he can be cruel, he is a wonderful man, a *prince*." She gave the last word its French inflection, which had the effect of making it seem to Dora a questionable compliment.

"You . . . you love him?" she asked helplessly.

"Ah, *mademoiselle*, unhappy soul that I am, I love him desperately," sobbed Yvette, gauging Dora's reaction out of the corner of her eye. "How crushed I was when he came to me to tell me it was over, and that you were to be my successor. How I hated you, for many days, until I realized that whatever I said or did nothing would change his mind. And so I determined that at the very least I would make certain you would care for him, *ma chère*, as I do. He is a difficult man, *mademoiselle*, sometimes a very cruel one—" she paused for dramatic effect and had the satisfaction of seeing Dora colour "—but he is very dear to me. I must be certain that you will not take what he offers you and turn away, for that would be to disgrace him before the ton, and he is a man of pride. It would kill him to be so used. And it would kill me to see him made unhappy."

"But I am afraid you've been misinformed after all, ma'am. I'm not going to be Mr. Carruthers's mistress, whatever he might have told you." Dora's head was reeling, but pride made her win the struggle to keep her voice calm. So this was the explanation of Carruthers's flattering manners toward a penniless companion! Dora had never suspected him of anything worse than a harmless flirtation, and she had even indulged the reckless hope—the stupid, idiotic hope—that he might have honourable intentions. But this! Dora looked around the overdecorated salon in distaste, imagining herself the hostess within these walls.

Could he really have such plans for her? A new thought stabbed at her. How else would Yvette know of Miss Thornfield's existence, let alone her tenuous connection with Carruthers, unless the gentleman had told her?

The weeping figure on the chaise longue made Dora's heart turn over in pity. This poor creature was to be turned out into the streets, and all so that the great Mr. Carruthers might indulge a whim. Dora imagined him deciding with a shrug that he might prefer a blonde to a brunette. He might even, she considered in horror, have thought it would be amusing to assist a prudish spinster down the primrose path!

"Please don't worry, Miss Yvette," Dora said softly. "Perhaps I can persuade him to take you back. I can tell you're devoted to him, and as I have no plans to become a— that is, I mean no disrespect to you, ma'am, but I already have a position, and kin to think of, so I couldn't become his . . . his . . ."

Yvette looked up again. "Doxy, *mademoiselle*? It is no shame to me to say the word. He is to marry, they say, a very young girl with money. It is the way of the world." She gave a noisy sigh, observing the shock on her guest's face at the tale that Carruthers was to marry that young thing. This woman's cousin, according to report. No harm in stirring up some jealousy there. "Well, we each of us must live our own life. But you must not mention me to Carruthers, *mademoiselle*. If he ever knew I had spoken to you he would beat me to within an inch of my life!"

"He would beat you?" gasped Dora in horror.

"*Oui*." Sitting up, Yvette pulled down the shoulder of her gown to reveal a large, purple bruise marring the satin skin of her upper arm. "He has a temper, as you can see, but ah, he can be an angel!" And she gave a romantic sigh.

The sight of the bruise turned the trick. Dora was shocked into silence for the moment. What an ugly world it was! Obviously this poor woman had a warped temperament, but even so, how could she still call desirable a man who did physical harm one moment and was an "angel" the next? Dora shuddered in revulsion at this new evidence of Carruthers's troubled nature and replied very gently, "Don't be afraid, ma'am. I never plan to speak to Mr. Carruthers again."

"Is your mother alive?" Yvette suddenly demanded.

Puzzled by this unexpected question, Dora replied, "No, she's been dead for many years."

"Then swear to me on the grave of your *maman* that you will never tell Laurent I spoke to you," demanded Yvette in her most dramatic tones.

Touched by the ring of fear in the woman's voice, Dora cried, "Yes, I swear, on anything you like. I will never tell him I saw you. Now I must go, ma'am. Good luck."

And, totally embarrassed by the proceedings and astonished that her predominant emotion toward this woman of easy virtue should be pity, not disgust, Dora fairly ran from the room, past the wooden-faced butler and out the front door. Only when she was safe on the pavement of Charles Street did she pause a moment to allow the rapid beating of her heart to calm.

In the house, Yvette was gazing with complacency at the artistic bruise she had created. Her most important little touch. She was glad she had remembered to make the spinster swear never to tell Carruthers what she had seen and done this day. Such a creature would never break a solemn vow. Well, the problem of Miss Thornfield was now settled, or Yvette missed her guess, and she didn't think it would be necessary to call off the plain young debutante, Miss Thornfield's cousin. She had watched Carruthers with the chit, and she couldn't believe there were any intentions in that direction at all.

Readjusting the neckline of her gown, Mademoiselle Yvette stared off into space. There was no telling where this boldness would lead her. His "respectable" plans in ruins, would Carruthers return to her? There was a chance, but it was only that. If he did not fall prey to Yvette's wiles, what would she do? She was getting on in years. Time was running out.

The next tears to fall from Yvette's eyes were genuine, as she sat in her ornate room and contemplated the future, an exercise she never indulged in if she could help it.

DORA SPED to the shops, the brisk walk helping no end to calm her wayward thoughts and return her to something resembling a normal condition. With conscious deliberation she chose the ribbon Lady Bracken required and then made her way home, thinking all the while of Carruthers's perfidy. How she hated the man! To think of him beating that poor creature! And planning to make her, Dora, his mistress.

She was only a few houses from home when the very demon of her thoughts issued forth from the Bracken front door and came toward her along the pavement. Carruthers! Never had he looked so happy, so carefree. Men! He recognized her from afar and smiled. His step quickened.

"Miss Thornfield! I'm lucky indeed to have the pleasure of seeing you after all. I've been making my formal invitation to Lady Bracken for the Thursday excursion down to Buckinghamshire, and I was naturally disappointed at your absence."

His manner was frank, his voice happy and excited. Genuinely pleased to see her, he seemed. How Dora would have thrilled to this encounter a mere hour before!

Now, she did the only thing she could do. Meeting his eyes for the briefest of moments, she averted her face and stepped around him to continue on her way. It was the cut direct.

Lawrence Carruthers was so astonished at this treatment from the lady that he merely stared after her. Even when he realized that she must have some bee in her bonnet and it would behoove him to know what, he let her go. He had seen the stern set of Miss Thornfield's jaw and the steely expression in her hitherto soft grey eyes. His experience with women had taught him that it was best to let them cool down before approaching them with questions and, if need be, abject apologies.

CHAPTER TEN

WHEN THE HUGE BOUQUET of white roses in a pretty Wedgwood vase arrived later that afternoon, dragged up to the modest bed chamber by a nearly fawning chambermaid, Dora was half inclined to pitch the whole business out the window. Instead, she managed to accept the flowers graciously, thanking Betsy for taking the trouble.

"Oh, for such flowers, ma'am," cried the maid, the same one who had disdained to carry up Sir James Perry's modest floral offering, "I simply had to see your face. Isn't it wonderful?"

Dora agreed that the gift was, and as soon as she was alone—for luckily Betsy had to go about her duties and couldn't stay to chatter on about Dora's magnificent present—she plucked out the card clipped to the vase which set off the lush white blooms so perfectly. Carruthers's card. And scrawled on the back the words: "Whatever I have done, forgive me. Your devoted admirer, always your friend."

"How I hate that deceiving, conniving man!" burst out Dora, startled to hear the words echo in her little room. She hadn't realized she had spoken aloud.

She had grown to hate the perfidious Carruthers even more within the hour, when news of the showy bouquet had spread through the house, bringing Lady Bracken's curiosity down upon Dora with a vengeance.

Summoned to her ladyship's sitting room, Dora was forced to admit that a large number of roses had indeed been delivered to her.

Lady Bracken's eyes were keen. "The servants didn't mistake the name on the card, then? I would be very willing to believe that such a thing should have been sent to my Augusta. Such a popular girl, is she not? But they were really for you! My dear, I must congratulate you! Sir James Perry has never been known to be so generous. Why, though I wouldn't think of repeating gossip, I once heard his late wife style him a miserable old squeeze-penny. Well! The happy hour of the declaration must be upon you." She smiled archly.

Dora merely nodded, knowing what a calamity would befall her if it became known that Mr. Carruthers, not Sir James, had been the generous giver.

"Oh, Dora," cried Augusta, bursting into the room at this point, "I simply had to go up to your room to see them. What a delightful present! There must be four dozen of them, Mama, and the Wedgwood vase! I've never seen anything so elegant."

"Sir James is indeed kind," her mother affirmed. "But perhaps he's being just a wee bit selfish? He might reasonably expect the vase to be displayed in his own home before many weeks have passed—in his wife's boudoir, perhaps?"

Dora, through a great effort of will, remained silent.

It had obviously been on the tip of Augusta's tongue to ask next who Dora's admirer was. At mention of the prosy and red-nosed Sir James, her face fell, and she was soon excusing herself to dress for the evening.

"I ought to be doing the same," Lady Bracken said, rising with a gentle stretch. "Cousin, you matched that ribbon perfectly today; I had no chance to tell you before. And if you'd be so good as to sew it onto my gown now? In a lover's knot, to match the others? You have so much more leisure than my poor dresser, for I'll be needing Meeker now, and it will be pleasant for you to sit in your room with Sir James's flowers while you do the work.''

"To be sure, ma'am," Dora said in a stiff voice. She collected the gown and ribbon and strode from the room without another word, leaving Lady Bracken to meditate on her companion's surliness, and to look forward, with mixed pleasure, to the day she would have to acknowledge her cousin as an equal when she became Lady Perry.

FOR THE NEXT FEW DAYS Dora lived very quietly. Lady Bracken, believing that it would be best for Augusta's interests to keep a very short rein indeed on Cousin Theodora, saw to it that her own health permitted her to keep all engagements, thus denying Dora the duty of acting as Augusta's chaperone. To Dora she allowed, with a titter, that a woman ought to keep her mystery, and that Sir James Perry would be all the more ardent for being denied the sight of her.

"Besides, I have laid my plans for the next time you see the dear man to be a very romantic occasion indeed. The countryside in spring, my dear. What could be more conducive to a declaration?''

Dora, recognizing the reference to the famous rural excursion to Carruthers's estate of Ashvale—and Thursday was fast approaching—knew that Mr. Carruthers disliked Sir James and would never invite him on such an intimate outing. Besides, she was absolutely determined not to go herself.

The days of relative solitude, banished as she was to the upper floors when callers came and excluded from parties, were a welcome respite to Dora, in the main. Even Amelia Lavenham had had to go out of town, on a flying visit to an elderly relative. Dora had nothing but time to think over Carruthers's villainy, and as an added benefit, she wasn't once constrained to see the man. Cutting him in the street and refusing to acknowledge his bouquet of flowers had been difficult enough, but she would die if forced to sit down to dinner or cards with Lawrence Carruthers before her rage had cooled.

The only thing in which she was unsuccessful was begging off the journey to Buckinghamshire. Lady Bracken could not have agreed more at first with Cousin Theodora's sensible wish to remain at home; but even she changed her mind in the ensuing days and for some odd reason insisted that Theodora go on the excursion.

That reason became clear on the night before the trip. Dora, having seen the others off to Almack's had retired to her room where she spent a solitary evening reading, mending and asking herself how in heaven's name she was going to be civil to her host on the morrow. What if he...horrors, what if he should ask to make her his mistress? A country outing might be the very place to come by the privacy necessary for the offer of a *carte blanche*. Perhaps the horrid man would even think a declaration of such revolting intentions would please her! He knew only that she was angry with him for some reason, not that she had learned the whole of his black plan from Yvette.

What with this fretting and stewing, Dora was still restless long after midnight. She lighted some candles and opened the novel she had been trying to read earlier.

There was a tap at the door, and at Dora's surprised "Enter," Augusta popped her head in.

"I saw your light," the young girl whispered, coming in and shutting the door carefully behind her. "Oh, Dora, I'm afraid Mama's done it!"

Dora looked her question. She was sitting in a comfortable chair beside the table that held her candles, and she motioned Augusta to the place opposite her, the only other seat in the room.

Augusta ignored this and bounced onto the bed instead. "Well," she said importantly, in the style of one of the gossiping dowagers she had no doubt observed, "who should we meet at Almack's but Mr. Carruthers."

"Indeed?" asked Dora, patting back a yawn.

"Yes, and by the way, he asked after you. He told me to tell you he's willing to go to any lengths if you'll give over being vexed at him, and so of course I told him you're never vexed with anyone, and he must have mistaken your intent."

"Did he say anything else?" Dora couldn't help enquiring, though she tried to make her voice neutral.

"Well, no, he merely smiled. But you haven't heard the dreadful part. While Mr. Carruthers was still with us, that ghastly Sir James came up to us with his dreadful daughters—that Alice is exactly like a horse!—and Mama gushed and went on so about Mr. Carruthers's party to Ashvale tomorrow that Mr. Carruthers was positively constrained to invite them."

"Sir James and his daughters?" choked Dora. Tomorrow's event, besides being the first time she would be forced to look on Carruthers's face since the day Yvette had told her of his profligacy, now loomed as a hellish outing with the Perry family.

Augusta, looking very sympathetic, reaffirmed that this was the case. "I felt so sorry for you," she sighed, "for I know how it will be. And I could swear Mama had the whole thing planned beforehand! It's too bad of her."

"No wonder she won't let me cry off," muttered Dora. "Well, thank you for the warning, dear."

Augusta, with a conspiratorial air, kissed Dora good-night and, before going to her own room, urged her cousin not to dread the morrow too much. If Sir James could but be fobbed off somehow, it promised to be a wonderful day! Augusta was so very anxious to see Buckinghamshire.

Dora noticed that the girl did seem excited about something, more excited than an ordinary social engagement would warrant. And why on earth should the girl have a particular desire to see that area of the country? Unless she were hoping to live there one day herself?

WHEN DORA ROSE on the fatal morning, she first considered retiring to bed and sending a message to Lady Bracken stating that she had the headache. Then she chided herself for such cowardice, for she would have to face Carruthers sooner or later, and it might as well be today. As for Sir James, it might be good if he did offer his heart and hand, for she would refuse him and that whole wretched interlude would be over.

Next, Dora debated wearing her plainest and most unbecoming things to forestall the ardour—illicit or decorous—of either gentleman. Despite her sister Mary's attention to her wardrobe, she did still own a very unstylish brown pelisse, not to mention a plain straw bonnet she used to wear at home while working in the herb garden. But no, such a scheme was unworthy of her. Feeling very virtuous, Dora finally arrayed herself in her best pelisse and a new bonnet, trimmed with one rose under the brim. A quick glance in the mirror and she was ready for the slaughter.

Shaking her head at her own nervousness, Dora tripped bravely down the stairs to do battle with all the dragons she might encounter on this most inauspicious of days.

CHAPTER ELEVEN

THREE HOURS LATER, Dora was wondering if anything good could ever be salvaged from the ruin of this day. To her horror, she had found herself pushed into a coach with the Perry party for the ride out to Buckinghamshire, which it might have been possible to enjoy, given the lovely day and the well-sprung, if lumbering, Perry post-chaise. Instead the trip was a purgatory. Caroline and Alice Perry giggled and chattered, and Sir James, placed next to Dora, leered and pretended to regret that the girls' aunt, his sister, had had to stay at home.

At journey's end, Dora stepped out of the coach and without thinking gave a radiant smile to the person handing her down. Her ears were ringing from the latest of twenty anecdotes involving the "motherless little ones at home," and her eyes—which were a tiny bit weak—had not yet become accustomed to the bright daylight after the dim interior of the chaise.

"Well! I'm delighted to see you, too, Miss Thornfield," Mr. Carruthers said, and Dora was shocked to realize that she had had the misfortune to give him her arm, and her smile. She briefly scanned his pleased face. Then immediately she put on her coldest expression, nodded and turned from him to take in her surroundings. The gentleman looked stricken, but he soon put his smile back on and moved to the other guests.

The massive house of Ashvale had a delightful classical façade, only a series of projecting bay windows marring its simplicity. And as for the park the visitors had just driven through! It seemed to go on for miles, a fairyland of rolling green dotted with fine old oaks, with deer grazing here and there. Dora's observation of the park was all mixed up in her mind with the missing front tooth of a small Perry boy, which delightful anecdote Caroline Perry had been reciting for the last half hour, but she wished very much she might walk about these fine, gracious grounds. Alone.

Carruthers's lady guests had come out in carriages, with the gentlemen for the most part riding horseback. The Perry party was the last to arrive. Standing on the front steps now, admiring the prospect of a small Greek folly that could be glimpsed through the spring foliage at a little distance, was the rest of the gathering. Lady Bracken was talking to Captain Laughton, and Augusta was with two women whom Dora had never seen before and whom she assumed were Edgar Farley's mother and sister.

The giggling female Perrys swooped down on Augusta and drew her aside for some excited chitchat, while Sir James, puffing his way out last of all from his carriage, clamped a hand on Dora's arm.

"Ah, my dear Miss Thornfield," said Sir James. "How I long to show you *my* seat one day."

Dora inclined her head coldly and, disengaging her arm, walked up to Mr. Farley, who had been standing to one side looking rather forlorn.

The young man's eyes brightened at sight of Miss Thornfield's smiling face. "Ma'am, I'm glad to see you! No chance in getting a word with Augusta, now that she's busy with those girls." His smile faded as he observed those girls' father hurrying up behind Dora.

Dora understood the look. "The Perry sisters are certainly lively," she said, with a smile at Sir James. "I'm sure all three young ladies would welcome you in their midst, Mr. Farley."

"Well, er..." Edgar ran a finger inside his collar and coughed, perfectly expressing his reluctance to ally himself with a gaggle of females. "May I introduce you to my mother and sister, ma'am? And Sir James."

Dora found her arm once more captured by the plump hand of Sir James, and in self-defence she grasped Mr. Farley's elbow. They walked across the front steps to where Mrs. Farley and her daughter, Selina, had been standing.

Miss Selina Farley, whose age Dora put at about thirty-five, looked a great deal like her brother, dark-eyed and serious. She was dressed in quiet, plain country clothing. Her mother, a stout lady in perhaps the middle sixties, wore a widow's cap and similarly un-tonnish garb. There was an aura of honesty and freshness about both women which Dora appreciated the more for having spent some time in the snobbish circles of the ton.

"Sir James," said Selina Farley with a friendly nod, "we were just noticing, Mama and I, those two charming girls, Augusta Bracken's friends. They're your daughters, I believe?"

The baronet could never resist a compliment on his children. Admitting that the girls belonged to him, he launched on an involved tale of their successful season.

Luckily for Dora, who had heard it all before and had to pity the Farleys for being forced to listen to Sir James's rambling, Mr. Carruthers called the party together and made general introductions. Sir Giles and Lady Bracken, Captain Laughton, and the three young girls were collected from their various places on the front sweep and the steps, and the group went through the front portico and into a charming Great Hall, lined with a carved wooden gallery. Far above the heads of the company was one of the features of the house mentioned in the guide book: a lovely illusionistic ceiling, rimmed with stuccoed mythological figures framing a centre painted to look as though it curved into a dome.

"How lovely!" exclaimed Dora.

"So glad you approve, ma'am," said Mr. Carruthers from directly behind her. Ignoring the lady's violent start and subsequent cold stare, he continued, "My house is somewhat eclectic, but I find it a happy mixture of every style from the Elizabethan—this hall—to the Italian ceiling that was my grandfather's favourite improvement. Now, may I introduce you and the other ladies to the housekeeper?"

Dora and the other females of the party were given into the hands of Mrs. Taverner, a stout, motherly woman, and taken upstairs to refresh themselves. Dora noticed, as they mounted the staircase and she was given an opportunity to see the gentlemen milling about below, that the numbers were uneven. How like a man! she thought indulgently before she remembered that fond thoughts of a gentleman whose depravity had sunk to the depths of Carruthers's were not at all appropriate.

When the ladies were fussing and refurbishing in the bedroom and sitting room laid aside for their use, Dora, who had been set to mending a nearly invisible tear in the hem of Lady Bracken's pelisse, was able to observe what an effort her cousin Maud was putting forth to conceal her irritation at the Farleys' presence. Though she found it hard to be civil to these neighbours of hers from Surrey—interlopers at what amounted to Augusta's party!—she found them useful nevertheless, for they were a mine of information about acquaintances she had lost track of since her own

arrival in town. However, in spite of her ladyship's best efforts it was more than obvious that she was not pleased that
Carruthers had invited his indigent relations—including that
tiresome boy, Edgar!—along on this jaunt. On hearing they
were actually Carruthers's guests in town, her eyes rolled
heavenward, and she felt obligated, for everyone's comfort, to clarify the situation.

"Wasn't it sweet of Mr. Carruthers to arrange this
party?" she said in a loud whisper to her professed friend,
Mrs. Farley. "My Augusta is so thrilled at the thought of
seeing his estate, for who can tell, dear ma'am, when she
might be making a very extended stay here?"

Mrs. Farley stared, and her eyes flickered from the brown-
haired young girl, whom she had known from the cradle, to
the young lady's complacent-looking mama. She finally
made a noncommittal murmur, and Dora, observing this
exchange, concluded that Mrs. Farley would be surprised if
Carruthers married Augusta. But Dora could believe anything of him now; it wasn't easy to imagine what the
gentleman would do next. A marriage to a seventeen-year-
old chit was as likely as anything.

Carruthers had arranged for luncheon to be served in an
airy parlour at the back of the house, a room with high,
arched windows and massive old furnishings that gave the
feeling of a mediaeval castle. "The windows and the deco-
rations were an innovation of my romantic mother's," he
explained when the ladies went into raptures.

"Dear Lady Anne," sighed Mrs. Farley, and she held the
floor for a while with reminiscences of that sterling woman.

Lady Bracken was unused to being anything but the centre
of attention in a setting where she ranked highest, and she
was also less than thrilled at the thought of her impecu-
nious neighbour from Surrey being the intimate of people
of rank. Mrs. Farley was even Carruthers's hostess today,

rather than Lady Bracken, and as Carruthers's future
mama-in-law the latter lady couldn't but feel a bit ill-used.
Only the knowledge that the Farley woman was related to
the gentleman mollified her. "How I do long to wander over
these charming grounds," Lady Bracken soon said loudly
to put a period to Mrs. Farley's featured role. "Do you plan
to show us the house first, Mr. Carruthers, or the gardens?"

Carruthers turned to her and said, "Well, ma'am, this is
England and the sun is shining. What would you suggest?"

"Oh, the gardens!" cried Lady Bracken, and the others
wasted no time in agreeing.

Dora, wedged between Sir James and Captain Laughton,
could only hope that the tour wouldn't allow for any private interviews between any of the guests. She could sense
that Sir James was working up to a declaration with every
compliment to her bright eyes and delightful smile. Captain
Laughton, to do him credit, had been trying to deflect these
attentions as best he could. Still, the day was turning out to
be as uncomfortable as Dora had envisioned. At least Mr.
Carruthers's duties as host meant that he couldn't plague
her.

How dreadful to be the guest of a man one had so much
reason to distrust, Dora was thinking as the chattering group
struck out across a stretch of lawn. Mr. Carruthers said
there was a pretty view from a nearby crest. The Perry sisters had captured Dora again and were gabbling to her about
their older sister's fine estate. How Miss Thornfield would
love it! It was quite ten miles to the nearest village.

Dora had a mental picture of the second Lady Perry, accompanied by crowds of stepchildren, on a visit to her eldest daughter at an isolated spot in Shropshire. She
shuddered.

"Are you cold, Miss Thornfield?" asked Alice. "Let me run back and get you a shawl."

Dora hastened to assure her thoughtful companions that she was quite the thing.

Mr. Carruthers was leading the way, and Dora was disconcerted, to put it mildly, to find that his strong, muscular figure and handsome profile affected her as much as ever. How could she still be attracted to a man who so coldly planned to make her his mistress? Who had not scrupled to discuss that sordid situation with his former ladybird? Was she—Dora frowned in thought—could she be in love with such a dreadful man?

"'Therefore is wing'd Cupid painted blind,'" she muttered under her breath.

"What did you say, Miss Thornfield?" said Caroline Perry. Then, noticing the older lady's frown, the girl decided that entertainment, not questioning, was in order, and began another silly story about a bungling shopping trip she and Alice—so sorely in need of female advice—had taken the other day. Perhaps Miss Thornfield would care to accompany them sometime.

"Your aunt..." ventured Dora, still looking ahead at Carruthers. She noticed he had taken Augusta's arm.

"Oh, poor Aunt has no idea what's in fashion, nor does she care," Miss Alice said airily.

Dora let the girls chatter on, but she paid no more attention to them than to the twittering of the birds in the surrounding beech trees. Her eyes had turned, as if in empathy, to the only member of the party who was certainly suffering from unrequited love. Poor Mr. Farley! He must be miserable, now that Augusta was actually walking with the very gentleman Farley had most cause to fear as a rival.

Dora was somehow put off to see that Edgar Farley, far from pining, was talking quite happily to his sister, point-

ing out some interesting horticultural specimen by the side
of the brick path. Perhaps those stories about the resiliency
of youth had more truth to them than Dora supposed. She
must hope that a certain spinster of more mature years
would be as lucky in getting over her unsuitable infatua-
tion.

Carruthers and Augusta had halted at a sunny clearing
where the path seemed to end. As the others grew closer,
they saw that it was actually the crest of a hill, and that the
path continued down a gentle slope beyond a stile.

Putting one foot upon the stile, Carruthers said, "Well,
Miss Bracken, what do you think? There is the village of
Ashvale. Does it please you?"

Augusta smiled and blushed, and Lady Bracken, delighted at the turn things were taking, answered for her
daughter. "Oh, she is pleased speechless, sir! What a very
pretty village."

It was indeed a pretty village the others discovered when
they gathered round. An old church with a Norman tower
was the centre of a well-kept collection of thatched cot-
tages. The view from the hillside delighted the eye. "That
large house there, the stone building near the church, is the
parsonage," Carruthers continued.

"Charming," sighed Lady Bracken.

Someone else suggested a walk down the hillside to examine the church, whose tower, along with a certain font,
were quite worth seeing. Edgar Farley mentioned he had
heard of them.

It was all too much for Dora. Carruthers really was angling to marry Augusta, for why else should he make such
a public show of giving her first view of the village and
church?

"It's all quite sweet," was the only comment Augusta
made, with lowered eyes.

In the bustle of getting the women safely over the stile, Dora made a sudden decision. "I'm going back to the house, if I may," she said in a low voice to Lady Bracken.

"Oh, go along, dear, and I'm certain Sir James will want to escort you," her ladyship answered. "Are you feeling headachy?"

"Something like that," said Dora, still speaking quietly, "and I'm quite capable of getting back by myself."

Lady Bracken's voice was famous for its ability to carry across a room, and it had no difficulty in reaching Sir James Perry in the next moment. "Nonsense, cousin! Walk about unattended? I can't allow it. No, Sir James must be prevailed upon. Oh, sir!"

"My lady?" Sir James trotted up.

"Cousin Theodora has the headache. Please take her back to the house and place her into the hands of the housekeeper," Lady Bracken directed, over Dora's increasingly desperate protests.

"Ah, with pleasure, madam," replied Sir James. The others couldn't help noticing the little conversation, for Dora's pleas were becoming almost strident, and soon it had become a matter of general dispute who should take Miss Thornfield safely across the hundred or so yards of lawn and woods that separated her from the manor.

The Perry girls spoke out with all the cunning at their command for Papa's right to that honour. But Captain Laughton, with an amused look at the young ladies and a worried glance at Dora, offered himself as escort. Finally even Mr. Carruthers said he would take Miss Thornfield back and see her into the best sitting room.

Dora was near to screaming by now, and her headache had long since become a reality. "No, no, no!" she cried. "Nobody is to miss seeing the church on my account. I'll go with you, after all." This, she reasoned gloomily, was the surest way to avoid a tête-à-tête with Sir James.

Surprisingly Mr. Carruthers negated this idea. "Miss Thornfield, you have obviously overtired yourself, and we can't allow you to go traipsing about the countryside. I'll take you back. Now."

His voice rang with authority, and despite such reactions to his plan as Sir James's and Captain Laughton's scowls of jealousy, Lady Bracken's shocked intake of breath and the Perry girls' giggling assertions of Papa's prior claim, he tucked Dora's hand securely beneath his arm and marched away from the group. "Cousin Edgar, I know you're an expert on old churches, and I delegate leadership of this expedition to you," he called over his shoulder. "Take Miss Bracken's arm. That's right. I'll be with you all as soon as I see Miss Thornfield settled."

Dora, trapped by the man she had most reason to fear, merely shivered as she and her escort got farther away from the others and nearer to an ominous privacy.

Carruthers was not one to mince words. "Now that I've got you alone, ma'am, perhaps you'd be good enough to tell me what I've done to offend you so mortally."

Dora sneaked a look up at him. The handsome face was regarding her with honest concern. Honest! That was a laugh. But she must remember that, whatever she now knew about him thanks to the good offices of Yvette, in his eyes she had merely become vexed with him for an unfathomable feminine reason.

"Mr. Carruthers," she said, striving for Christian charity, "I'm very sorry I cut you in the street that day. The flowers you sent were a flattering attention and I was at fault for not acknowledging your lovely gift before now. Can't we leave it at that?"

"Without your telling me what's wrong? Why the lovely lady I once knew to smile upon me from time to time has turned into an iceberg? And then there's the matter of your recent seclusion. I can hardly believe that you've been absenting yourself from parties merely to avoid seeing me. Well? I'm going to have to demand an answer, Miss Thornfield." Coming to a halt on the pathway beneath a very picturesque oak in new leaf, Carruthers faced Dora in determination.

She peeked up into his face from beneath her bonnet's poke, alarmed at her own dazzled reaction to the mere fact of his nearness. "I—I've been staying in a lot for various reasons, none of which have to do with you," she stated, avoiding his main question.

"And you won't tell me what I've done." Carruthers stared down at her keenly. She looked very embarrassed, and this suddenly led him to understand that, whatever he had done to displease her, she couldn't bring herself to talk about it. Carruthers had an elevated notion of Dora's modesty that would have made the lady herself laugh had she but known of it. He had been treading on eggs to avoid making his attentions too obvious, for he didn't want to scare her off. The large bouquet of roses had been a rare lapse, one which he was anxious to repeat if only she would give him the word. He made a decision. "Well, let's leave it unsaid, as you wish. But, whatever it was, will you forgive me and begin our friendship anew?"

Now Dora was in a dreadful predicament. There was a solid, brown hand held out to her and she longed to take it, forget she had ever met that creature Yvette, and cry friends. But how could she, knowing that at any moment Carruthers might try to seduce her?

Carruthers took her hesitation for assent and reached out to capture her hand. Impulsively he stripped off her rose-coloured kid glove, pocketed it and planted a lingering kiss on Dora's palm.

She shuddered with some emotion she couldn't identify.

And Carruthers, having felt that response, rushed his fences. "My love, I've tried to be patient, to wait for the proper moment, but I can't. I must have you. My darling—" And crushing Dora to him, he kissed her, tenderly at first, then with a demanding passion that seemed to wrest a response from his astonished partner.

She pulled back, though, as soon as his embrace slackened enough to allow her escape. "Sir!" she whispered. She felt weak. The limbs that had seemed to sing with life a moment before might now be full of water for all the assistance they were in supporting her.

"Please say it. Say you want me, too," he murmured, lips wandering over her cheeks and forehead and throat before returning to her mouth, which he had no hesitation in covering with his own, though he had just demanded an answer from her.

Moaning and shaking her head, Dora wriggled out of his grasp. Who would have thought the offer of a *carte blanche* could be such an unsettling, tempting situation? She was ashamed of herself, and she blamed this horrid man for her weakness. Resolutely she pushed her hands against his chest. "No," she ground out, not looking into his eyes. "How dare you? I'd never have believed you would really ask this of me, Mr. Carruthers. Have you no shame, no delicacy at all?" Her last words ended on a sob and she ran down the path toward the house, wild to get away from him.

Carruthers's eyebrows knotted together in a scowl. How did he dare? What the devil? She was not the ordinary spinster, he would say that for her: melting in his arms one moment, accusing him of indelicacy the next. "Teasing jade!" he shouted after her. Then, recollecting where he was, he snapped his mouth shut and stalked back in the other direction. He didn't doubt that Miss Thornfield would find a comfortable spot to rest in the house. What he did doubt was that he would ever willingly go near the woman again.

A moment's reflection led him to remember that she was an innocent and that she'd lived retired in the country for many years. She could have had little experience of male ardour; no wonder it had shocked and disgusted her. He would beg her pardon for this latest offence and press for an answer to his question. She ought to have cooled down by now. He turned and retraced his steps.

DORA HAD SNEAKED into the house through some French doors and was ensconced in a leather library chair. She was trembling. How could he? But more important, how could she? The mere touch of his lips and hands had caused her to seriously consider casting away her respectability and do as he'd asked: become his mistress. Dora was nearing thirty, and all she knew of physical intimacy came from the experiences of her sisters, who were all married, all with children. Dora had somehow thought of married life as one endless pregnancy, punctuated only briefly by the odd, shadowy acts that induced the state. She had not thought that her sisters found such acts enjoyable. And never had she considered that such very indecorous desires could surge through her own virginal veins. What would it be like to know him intimately? her traitorous body demanded. Finally to learn the secrets of the marriage bed, though not in marriage, tutored by that lean, hard-muscled body, those brutal lips...? It would be a delight.

Unfortunately it would be a wrong greater than Dora was willing to commit, considering that she had to live in the world and with herself. She sighed. She had better accept Sir

James Perry as soon as he offered and make sure the honeymoon took her as far from Mr. Carruthers as humanly possible.

The library door crashed open and there *he* stood. She might have known he wasn't finished with her. "The servants told me you'd come in here, my dear." Carruthers advanced into the room and knelt before Dora's chair, forestalling her attempt to rise and rush out of the room. He grasped her hands. "I'm sorry about what just happened. I promise not to hurry you. But your promise I must have. Please, my dear. Your kisses tell me you could learn to care, if you don't already. May I . . . may I start to make plans?"

"Plans!" Dora was startled into animation. She forced herself to look anywhere but into his warm hazel eyes, for she suspected they were aglint with lust. "How can you, sir, when I've just refused to have anything to do with your lewd designs, dare to break in on me again and suggest plans! I happen to know that you already have the practical arrangements of your liaisons well in order. You...you beast. Please don't follow me again." And she managed to extricate herself from the chair with only one burning touch of her leg against Carruthers's shoulder. She stalked from the room and slammed the door behind her.

Carruthers was left staring after her, half-bemused, half-angry, and completely astonished.

"Lewd designs?" he repeated in consternation. He got to his feet, made for the door and then, thinking better of another encounter with that prickly female, settled himself into the chair she'd vacated. It was still warm. Carruthers stayed there until he finally remembered his guests, whereupon he wandered back outside to find them and continue the day's somewhat unusual entertainment.

CHAPTER TWELVE

DORA RUSHED UPSTAIRS to the sitting room that had been set aside for the ladies' comfort, and after a brief bout of tears and a rather unsuccessful attempt to compose herself, she went to the large bay window and looked out over the lawn. There was Mr. Carruthers, presumably on his way back to join the rest of the party. She could see him disappearing into the ornamental wood. She was safe at last from his insulting attentions.

Why, then, did she feel so lonely? Brushing this thought away, Dora went about the important business of having a headache. She rang for the maid and ordered a tisane, then took off her outdoor things and her shoes and lay down upon a sofa near the fire, all the time trying to banish from her distressed mind the teasing image of Lawrence Carruthers murmuring, "Tell me you want me."

To Dora's surprise, the hot draught she had ordered was brought, not by the maid, but by the elderly housekeeper, Mrs. Taverner.

"Mr. Carruthers said as how I was to see specially to all the ladies' comfort, ma'am," explained that worthy woman, bustling about to settle a small table near Dora, put a pillow at her back and feel her forehead quite in the manner of a sickroom nurse.

"How kind of your master," Dora said politely.

"Now you drink this right down, madam." Mrs. Taverner poured out the infusion into a Sèvres cup and eyed Dora severely.

As the lady was drinking her medicine, Mrs. Taverner apparently felt that the formalities were out of the way. "Yes, our Mr. Carruthers is a very kind man," she responded to Dora's earlier comment, folding her hands in front of her. "A good master, as his father was before him. I came to the house as a chambermaid, you know, ma'am, under his mother, Lady Anne, may she rest in peace."

"I suppose Mr. Carruthers was the usual naughty little boy who turned out well," Dora remarked, not without a touch of sarcasm.

Mrs. Taverner didn't notice this satirical inflection. "Oh, yes, Master Lawrence was the veriest little devil."

"Somehow I'm not shocked to hear that," answered Dora.

"And now he's the best master in the world! So thoughtful, such a generous soul. Ah, the only thing we have to wish for now is a mistress," Mrs. Taverner went on. She smiled meaningly at Dora. "Perhaps you can see to that problem, ma'am, if I might be so bold."

Dora doubted very much that the sort of mistress Carruthers intended her to be was ever brought to live in an ancestral home. But she understood that the sharp eyes of Mrs. Taverner might have noticed Mr. Carruthers's distinguishing her since their arrival—and misinterpreted it. Why, he was probably at this very moment declaring his hand and heart to Augusta! "I don't know what you mean," she responded in her most prim, most dismissive tones.

"Ah, such a modest young woman you are! But—" seeing Miss Thornfield's black frown, the housekeeper prudently decided to say no more "—you'll forgive me for the liberty, ma'am, and I'll keep my tongue between my teeth and leave you to take your rest."

Dora smiled kindly. "Thank you."

But when Mrs. Taverner had bustled out, Dora couldn't sleep no matter how hard she tried. Carruthers's lips on hers was all she could think of, and she promised herself again that she would accept Sir James Perry at once. Such a marriage ought to erase the memory of Carruthers. If nothing else, its nuisance value would be considerable, and that would preoccupy her.

The unwelcome thought struck her that no doubt Sir James would expect certain wifely duties which she was by no means anxious to perform. What on earth was to be done about that? Modesty and faked headaches would not see her far past the wedding night, and then what would she do? Allow those stubby hands of Sir James Perry's to roam over her body, as she had just, wickedly, been imagining those of Carruthers's doing?

"I will cross that bridge when I come to it," Dora said stoutly to herself, and feeling rather heartened by the knowledge that at least one man in the world honestly wanted to marry her—for whatever practical reason—she decided to go downstairs. Quite a bit of time had passed since she'd lain down, though she hadn't spent it sleeping, and the others ought to be returning from the village shortly.

Not expecting to meet anyone as yet, Dora strolled through the wide, elegant halls, where landscapes by Canaletto and Constable alternated with groups of family portraits. It was so difficult to imagine her little cousin Augusta mistress of all this. But Carruthers must intend the girl to be. Why else should he care what she, in particular, thought of the village and church? Shaking her head at the sad truth of this, Dora traversed the Great Hall, heading for the large chamber where the party had taken luncheon. She meant to wait there until some of the group wandered in.

As she was about to walk through the heavy, carved double doors, which had been left ajar, Dora was startled to hear a familiar voice. Augusta's!

"Oh, sir, I feel so badly about deceiving Mama and Papa," sighed the girl.

Dora halted where she was. Decency demanded that she turn on her heel and leave Augusta to have her conversation in private. But something held her motionless—curiosity, or was it only a lack of real scruples? She simply had to hear to whom Augusta was speaking.

"My dear girl, don't give it another thought. It was you who assured me that they must not know anything about our arrangement." The deep, intimate voice, lowered but audible, was that of Carruthers's.

"But I've been so very bold—sometimes I'm ashamed of myself." Augusta's next words made her eavesdropping cousin's heart turn over in pity. The cad! He was trifling with this young thing's heart, too! Had he—? Horrors, had the damage already been done?

Carruthers's answer confirmed this in Dora's resentful and prejudiced mind. "You did only what was entirely natural under the circumstances," he assured the girl in soothing tones. "Never be ashamed. You were motivated by love, and though I agree that your mama wouldn't understand, I do. Perfectly."

"Oh, Mr. Carruthers, you've already proven that," sighed Augusta.

This was too much for Dora. Flinging back the doors, she stalked into the room, her grey eyes ablaze and her hands clenched into fists. There she found the two partners in this shameful tête-à-tête: not embracing, thank goodness, but sitting in adjacent chairs at the now cleared dining table.

"Augusta!" declared Dora in her most regal manner. "You must never be alone with this dreadful man."

"Dora!" The girl jumped up. "Did you hear?"

"Enough," replied her cousin. A note of disgust was clearly audible in her tone.

"Oh! Promise you won't tell," Augusta begged, tears starting in her eyes.

"Dear, how can you doubt it? Of course I'll keep your secret. We will see what can be done. But Augusta, do you realize how very wrong you've been?" Dora's voice was gentle now as she tried to reassure the stricken girl.

Apparently she didn't do very well. Augusta burst into sobs and ran from the room.

Carruthers had got to his feet in the meantime, his eyes seeking out Dora's.

His amused expression infuriated her, and she stared boldly into his face. "What can you be about, sir, to take advantage of such a young girl? Your behaviour to me might be explained, if not excused, since I'm no longer young and virtually without protection. But what possible reason could you have for seducing that child, the daughter of your friend? I can only hope you've merely been anticipating a legal union. Do I make myself clear?" Dora now saw herself the chivalrous protector of her wayward cousin. "It would be most unfortunate if news of this were to come to her father's ears. Though I fear for the child in the hands of a libertine such as yourself, I must hope you'll be kind to her," she added, wishing her voice would not shake so.

"The role of enraged relation becomes you, my dear," Carruthers managed. He seemed to be holding back a strong tendency to laugh, and this set Dora's back up so much that she had to restrain herself from slapping his face.

"Oh, if I were only a male relation of that poor, innocent girl's," she cried. "You'd be naming your seconds, sir."

"Such fire, such spirit," Carruthers marvelled, stepping forward. "Can this be our very correct, prudish Miss Thornfield?" There was a dangerous, nearly wild look in his eye. Suddenly, without warning, he reached out to snatch Dora in his arms and kiss her, with quite as much passion and energy as he had displayed earlier in the woods. "I see the fire isn't only in your words," he muttered when he released her.

Dora gasped. His grip on her had been so strong, so unbending, that her desperate efforts to free herself had been totally useless. How dared he? She'd walked in on him in the middle of intriguing with her cousin, and he responded by kissing *her*? The man was beyond all hope of redemption.

"You'll pay for this, you fiend," she snapped, backing a safe distance away. "I will not be your mistress, if you have forgotten that important detail. And, as a member of Augusta Bracken's family, I warn you that I expect to see an announcement of your engagement within the week, or I'll have to take steps." Though the thought of facing Sir Giles Bracken to acquaint him with his daughter's ruin was not a pleasant one, Dora resolved on the spot to do it, if she had to, without flinching.

"I can safely promise you that," Carruthers said. "An announcement of my engagement within the week. Is there anything else?" His voice was cheerful; his eyes still caressed her.

Dora backed farther away. "You will never come near me again," she demanded.

"That might conflict with your earlier request, my dear," Carruthers answered, maddening in his assurance.

Dora was as angry as she had ever been in her life. "You—you disgusting man! You know very well what I mean. Naturally, as a distant member of the family and an employee of Lady Bracken's, I will have the misfortune to see you now and again, but I . . ." She paused, on the point of snapping that she never wanted him to kiss her again and realized that wasn't the truth.

"But you . . . ?" Carruthers prompted, stepping toward her.

He might have guessed her thoughts! Dora knew there was only one thing to do, and she did it. She turned on her heel and stalked from the room.

How was she to deal with Augusta? Dora wondered as she hurried through the hall once more, not really knowing where she ought to go next. Should she seek out the guilty young lady and have some sort of a woman-to-woman talk? Or had Augusta been punished enough already for her folly? Being discovered had certainly overwhelmed her. No, perhaps the best course would be simply to stand by like a watchdog and see that Augusta married her seducer before many weeks had passed.

"Ah, dear lady." Sir James! He and his daughters were sailing down the hall from the other direction, blocking off the avenue of escape.

"Why, are you back from the village, then?" Dora asked unnecessarily, in a voice which she hoped was normal.

"Yes, indeed, and an interesting visit it was," Sir James said. Approaching Dora, he took her hand. "And I trust your little ailment is much improved?"

"Oh, it was nothing," Dora said with a shrug.

"We were just going upstairs to take off our outdoor things," Caroline said, with a meaning glance at her sister. "Perhaps Papa wants to tell Miss Thornfield all about the church. It was so very fine, ma'am. That charming Mr.

Farley was telling us that the font dates from at least a couple of hundred years ago.''

''I think he said twelfth century,'' corrected Alice. ''Well, Caroline is right, Papa can give you all particulars, Miss Thornfield. We'll be down shortly.''

Both young ladies were tittering awfully as they scampered away toward the front stairs.

''Mr. Carruthers has promised us a tour of this venerable old pile next, Miss Thornfield,'' said Sir James, releasing the hand which Dora had been trying to tug away for some time. ''Then an early dinner before we begin the drive back to Town. The perfect host.''

''Perfect,'' Dora managed, torn between laughter and tears. Sir James was leading her into a small, untenanted sitting room. The big moment was apparently at hand. She would promise within the next five minutes to become the second Lady Perry.

Sir James closed the door of the chamber carefully behind him, motioned Dora to the nearest chair and, without further ado, got down upon one knee. ''Dear lady, you can't have mistaken my attentions to you in the past weeks.'' His nose, not to mention his cheeks, seemed to grow redder with every word. ''Do let us name the day. How I long to see you established in my house, giving my children the tender care they so desperately need. Guiding my elder daughters in the perilous straits of society. Oh, and naturally, your beauty and charm warming my hours of leisure.''

Dora stared down at her portly suitor. An honest proposal. A way to forget the horrid, confusing demands Mr. Carruthers was making upon her heart and body. Now she must give Sir James her answer. Why couldn't she speak?

Her hesitation prompted her admirer to add, ''You are overwhelmed. How natural. Your modesty, Miss Thornfield, has always been one of your most endearing qualities, and I don't blame you for not knowing how to reply to an offer which must surprise you. But I assure you, my dear, that I am well able to take on the charge of a penniless bride."

Dora looked into his eyes. Now she knew exactly what to say. "Dear sir, I'm very honoured by your flattering interest in me, but I—I have no plans to marry."

Sir James stared. "What? But Miss Thornfield—consider what you are giving up." Rather clumsily, he got to his feet and took up a position with more dignity, in a chair opposite the lady's.

"You offer a great deal, Sir James. But I haven't the affection for you that a bride should bring to her husband."

The baronet's brow cleared. "Ah. But, my dear young lady, I don't expect anything of that sort. At our time of life what is most important between a wife and a husband, even in the more—er, intimate moments of marriage, is friendship and respect."

I don't have those for you, either! Dora wanted to wail, but she sensibly held her tongue for the moment. There was no use in insulting him.

"Now may I go to tell my daughters the happy news?" Sir James asked.

"But, sir, I've just refused you!" Dora protested. "And whatever my reasons are, I must insist that you respect them."

"Hmmph." Sir James looked into Dora's face and read her distress. "Well, I can see you're overset, my dear, but do allow me to hope. Another day, when you haven't been ill, you'll be more receptive. Ah, by the by, your health is, in general, robust, is it not? As the mother of a fine, hopeful family—with more to come, who knows?—you will need all your strength."

"I've hardly had a day's illness in my life," Dora was bound to admit, though she longed to tell some sort of lie about a chronic weakness of the lungs. "But my health won't be your concern, sir, I can promise you that.

"Yes, yes, we shall see." Sir James got to his feet and assisted Dora to hers. He was calm, unruffled, as though he proposed every day and was refused as often. Dora was terribly afraid his hopes weren't dashed. "Now shall we seek out the others? I would hate to compromise you into becoming my wife, dear Miss Thornfield." And, with a hearty laugh, Sir James led the way out of the room.

The Perry sisters hovered in the hall. "Papa!" they chorused. Both were smiling proprietarily at Dora. "What have you to tell us?"

"Nothing yet, my dears. I'll explain it all to you later," Sir James said with a cough and an uncomfortable glance at the lady by his side.

"Oh," said the girls, with downcast faces.

"Miss Thornfield isn't feeling well," elaborated Sir James, brightening suddenly. "She isn't strong enough for a serious talk."

"Oh." Caroline and Alice looked much happier.

Dora flashed an indignant look at her erstwhile cavalier. She supposed she ought to be grateful to him for forestalling the questions of his daughters by this little face-saving ruse. She didn't have the heart to contradict him and to admit to the Misses Perry that their papa had been rejected roundly. But perhaps something could be done to stop the gentleman's asking again. Dora was very certain now, as sure as she could be, that she couldn't run away from Mr. Carruthers by marrying Sir James. It would be bad enough to enter into a loveless marriage with the baronet—or anyone—if her affections weren't engaged elsewhere, but as she did have at least a physical attraction to that horrid, libertine gentleman, her host of the day, it would be madness to marry Sir James. It would, in fact, be a grievous wrong. No, it was spinsterhood for her, at least until she could wipe out all thoughts of Carruthers. If she could bring a husband nothing else—and she had nothing of her own—she must at least go to any marriage of convenience heart-free.

The Perry girls were on either side of Dora now, taking each of her arms and being very solicitous. "Would you like to lie down again? A shawl? A glass of water? The salts in my reticule?" Dora was still assuring the helpful young ladies that she was perfectly fine as they entered the drawing room, where the party was to assemble for the tour of the house.

"Alice has such a fine singing voice," Caroline Perry said, settling Miss Thornfield in the best chair in the room, which happened to be very near the couch on which Mrs. Farley and her daughter were established. "I'll play for her. I'm sure a few songs would soothe you, ma'am."

Dora had heard Alice sing before, but she was too kind to contradict. She stayed where she had been put, rejoicing a little in the fact that the drawing room of Ashvale was so very large that the pianoforte was far removed from her place. And Mr. Carruthers had not yet come in. That was a blessing.

"I do hope you're recovered, Miss Thornfield." It was Selina Farley speaking. "Those charming girls are so eager to assist you. How flattering."

Dora made a noncommittal sound and took a closer look at Miss Farley. She must be a very kind and congenial soul herself if she could call the Perry sisters charming. And she was so very attentive to her old mother. This indicated a child-loving nature. Dora's brain worked busily. Surely the establishment of Sir James Perry, baronet, could support an aged mother.

"Tell me, Miss Farley," she said with a smile, "are you fond of children?"

"Why, yes," answered the other lady, beaming. She had mild, dark, rather bovine eyes that radiated tenderness at the thought of little ones.

"I believe Sir James Perry has a very large family," Dora continued, feeling as though she should be slyer, but not knowing how. "Perhaps you could get the dear girls to tell you some of their stories of the nursery. They are so entertaining!"

"My Selina is fond of a good story," put in Mrs. Farley, over her spectacles.

"Good," said Dora. She and the elderly lady looked into each other's eyes. A flash of understanding passed between them while Selina obligingly glanced away.

The rest of the day was torture for Dora, for not only did she have to glare ferociously whenever Mr. Carruthers came near, she had to endure the tear-reddened face and timid looks of Augusta, who was obviously afraid that Dora would blurt out the whole story of the girl's seduction to her parents, promise or no. Then there were the clumsy gallantries of Sir James, and the high-handed commands of Lady Bracken, who sent her companion off twice after the same pair of gloves. These particular errands distressed Dora the more when she remembered her own kid glove, which Mr. Carruthers had put in his pocket earlier in the day. Though it was one of her best and she hated to lose it, she couldn't possibly ask for it back!

Captain Laughton managed to sit next to her at dinner, at least, and talk charmingly to her on everyday matters. "You are so very gallant, Captain," Dora said at one point, when he had actually succeeded in making her laugh.

Laughton was a very astute man. "I have a feeling you are glad to hear light chatter from a gentleman, Miss

Thornfield. It must be quite a change from some of what you have endured today.'' And he glanced significantly at Sir James, on Dora's other side.

She could respond only with a little smile.

"Then I am not to wish you happy?" Laughton asked.

"Heavens, no."

"And you aren't put off by a bit of light flirting from a man who admires you?"

The captain's tone was still joking, but Dora, in her mood of heightened emotion, tended to read more into his words than perhaps was there. She shrugged, declining to answer, and hoped that Captain Laughton wasn't working up to a proposal, too. She would hate to have to refuse him, so sweet and charming as he was. But she must remain steadfast in her determination to make no man unhappy, as any man must be who was saddled with a penniless wife in love with someone else.

What with Carruthers's proposition, Sir James's proposal and the discovery of Augusta's ruin, Dora had to call the excursion to Ashvale an utter failure. But she did accomplish one important thing that day. By dint of clever manoeuvring and some of the best excuses ever voiced, Dora saw to it that Miss Selina Farley rode back to London in the carriage of Sir James Perry.

CHAPTER THIRTEEN

LAWRENCE CARRUTHERS turned the corner into Charles Street much later on the night of his Ashvale party. The trip back to London had been accomplished without incident. The Bracken and Perry families, not to mention Captain Laughton, had departed to their respective homes, and the Farleys would at this very moment be tucking into a late supper at Carruthers's own house in Mount Street.

Bemused, Carruthers thought over the events of the day. Somehow Miss Theodora Thornfield was expecting him to announce his marriage to her cousin Augusta within the week. How this had happened, Carruthers could not really say. It had something to do with Miss Thornfield's unfortunate tendency to eavesdrop, not to mention her plaguey little cousin's blasted insistence on secrecy. Well, Carruthers trusted Augusta would make all clear to Theodora before much time had passed. It would certainly be better than allowing the lady to continue in her present confusion!

Remembering Dora's flashing grey eyes, her warm, pliant lips that had belied her words of hatred when pressed to his, Carruthers could not but think well of some of the day's happenings. He must give the lady a chance to cool and to talk to her cousin. The marriage announcement? In a few days he could take care of it. Now he put the intrigues of the day out of his mind to concentrate on the night at hand.

The butler admitted him, for Mr. Carruthers still paid the bills, but it was with a flash of surprise, and a footman was sent hurrying up the stairs to inform Mademoiselle of her visitor.

Carruthers raised his eyebrows as he was led into the rose salon, relieved of his hat and promised brandy within the next few moments. "Mademoiselle will come to you here, sir."

A sudden, devilish thought struck the caller, and he replied, "Ah, no need to disturb her to that extent. I'll simply go up to her boudoir. No, it's no trouble."

Farnham, the butler, startled into more animation than Carruthers had ever seen from the man, tried desperately to halt the gentleman's progress up the stairs. "Sir, my mistress will be desolated if I allow you to exert yourself. She will be down directly—sir!"

Paying no attention to the man scurrying along at his heels, Carruthers strode firmly down the upstairs hall, pausing before the door of the boudoir to announce loudly, "No, really, Farnham, it's no trouble at all. I'll go right in." Then, hesitating, he appeared to change his mind, but not for the better. "Come to think of it, Mademoiselle is bound to be abed at such an hour." He approached the next door down the hall and touched the handle.

Farnham, in a final heroic gesture, sprang past the gentleman and barricaded the door with his body. He stood staunchly, as though expecting to be shoved aside.

Carruthers was about to burst out laughing and retreat down the hall when the door opened behind the butler, making the man stagger, thus further trying Carruthers's sense of humour.

"Ah, Laurent," breathed Yvette in her silkiest voice, "I was coming down to you this instant."

She was looking very beautiful, if somewhat dishevelled, her wonderful hair hanging down her back, a rose-coloured, lacy robe casually draped about her body. She was breathing rather hard.

Carruthers smiled, his eyes raking over her in appreciation. "I'll come in. Much cosier, don't you think? Perhaps you'd give me a drink." Was that an inner door softly closing in the room behind her? Carruthers endeavoured to push past, and Yvette stood in his way for one nervous moment before she would let him enter.

"Ah, but yes, *mon cher*." Yvette made a show of giving the necessary orders to Farnham. Then she ushered her former protector into her pink-and-gold sanctum, which was decorated to match her boudoir and certainly rivalled it in gaudy splendour. "I am so surprised, Laurent," she remarked, inviting him to be seated on a sofa far away from the dishevelled bed, "but pleased." Her low, intimate tones gave no doubt of that. "Do you find the respectable world dull already?" She laid a flirtatious hand on his knee. There was a note in her voice that spoke vividly of hope, and Carruthers, who had burst into her bedroom on purpose to tease her, felt his heart soften. Poor Yvette.

"Save it, my love," advised her quarry, deftly removing her hand from his person. "I've come upon business of a sort. I hope your spark made it out the door, by the way, and isn't cowering behind those draperies. Most unnecessary, and it was unkind of me to interrupt."

Yvette flushed hotly and lowered her eyes.

"I know everything, you see," Carruthers continued, "and I've come for an explanation."

A gasp escaped the lovely woman beside him. "Everything? It means nothing to this so respectable spinster, then, to swear on the grave of her *maman*? Ah, *sacré bleu*, the good God save me from these creatures...."

Yvette descended into a flood of French invective, while Carruthers looked at her curiously. Why was her ire directed at an unnamed spinster? He had come to Charles Street this evening to inform Yvette that he had discovered in the evening mail notes from his banker and from Tattersall's. Yvette, it would seem, had been trading on his name for one last bauble: a carriage team. Carruthers, unable to countenance such continued generosity on his own part in light of the liberal settlement he had already made his mistress, had wished to warn the woman in person that her scheme hadn't worked, and that there had better not be others.

"Spinster?" he echoed, wondering if Coutts & Company now employed women.

"Revolting old maid! Treacherous *monstre*," clarified Yvette, lost in her own anger. So the mincing little beast, pretending to be so modest and shocked by the revelations of a courtesan, and so sincere in her promise not to repeat the conversation, had run straight to Carruthers! Now it would take all the guile Yvette possessed to get the man back. She began to wish she hadn't charged that team to him; but it had seemed so safe, since he would soon be coming back to Yvette in the wake of the Thornfield's rejection of his suit....

Carruthers shook his head. There was only one "spinster" on his mind these days. But this conversation could have nothing to do with Theodora. She could never have met Yvette, for the paths of the two women in London who were the most different from each other would never cross. Dora's words of earlier in the day came back to him. Hadn't she shouted at him that she wouldn't become his mistress? Hadn't she declared herself shocked, disgusted by his words of love? For some daft reason she had thought he'd been offering her a slip on the shoulder. He stared harder at Yvette, who had ceased her muttering and was merely looking stormy.

"What on earth have you done?" he asked, awe clear in his voice. He remembered at least one social occasion that both Yvette and Dora had attended: thanks to the masks, Yvette had stolen into Lady Lavenham's ball. Could she... would Yvette have dared to drop a word into Dora's ear about Carruthers's former proclivities, thus giving the woman a disgust of him?

Yvette was inwardly chiding herself. He didn't know! Like the fair woman she was, she mentally cancelled all curses she had directed toward the blonde spinster. Well, there was no harm done. Laurent would never guess that she had talked with a respectable woman. "I have done nothing," she said sulkily. She dashed one of the angry tears from her eyes, knowing that such a gesture was becoming to her.

"You have never met a lady by the name of Thornfield?" Carruthers persisted. It struck him that it was dangerous to mention Theodora's name to a possible enemy, but he shook off that feeling. The damage, if there had been any from this quarter, was already done.

Yvette laughed. "Ah, what a strange name is that for a lady."

"Naturally it's her surname," said Carruthers, allowing himself a smile. "The lady in question has recently expressed displeasure over certain of my moral attributes, and I thought she might have heard from you—"

"From me?" Yvette interrupted him with a shocked gasp. "I discuss anything with a respectable female? I meet very few of those, you know." She paused. "If this lady has heard of your activities, you must know, *chéri*, that there are few secrets among your ton."

"Quite." Carruthers, engaged in quaffing the last of his brandy, fixed a suspicious eye on his former ladybird. She wouldn't tell him if she had done anything, and respectful of her instinct for self-preservation, he couldn't really blame her. Getting to his feet, he frowned into Yvette's upturned, questioning face. "Well, never mind about the lady. I'll let you get back to what you were doing, ma'am." He laughed at Yvette's conscious blush and good-humouredly kissed her hand. His own was on the door before he remembered to fling back at her, "And by the way, if you wish a new carriage team, you'll have to take the purchase price from the funds I've already settled on you."

Carruthers strode down the hall, past the anxiously hovering servants. On an impulse he looked into Farnham's eyes as that individual held the front door for him. "May I stand you to a drink, my friend?"

The butler's eyes shifted from the footman on the stairs to the gentleman beside him. "Sir, I will reiterate to Mademoiselle your regards," he said loudly. Out of the side of his mouth he whispered, "Around the corner. Five minutes."

Carruthers went out into the cool night air, confident that Yvette had indeed done something odd, something Farnham considered worthy of note. Whether it had to do with Theodora Thornfield remained to be seen.

A WHILE LATER, having loosened Farnham's tongue with Blue Ruin and fattened his pockets, Carruthers made his way through the streets, alternately chuckling at Yvette's boldness and shaking his head at the shock all this must have been to Dora. But try as he would, he couldn't really blame Yvette for anything she had done. It was flattering to oneself, in a way.

He trusted that Yvette's lover, whoever he was, had waited and had by now returned to the woman's side. Poor Yvette deserved some amusement, if she didn't merit unlimited access to the Carruthers funds. As he went on his way home, Carruthers dwelled on the delicious, dishevelled vision of Yvette as she had looked when she had opened the bedroom door. There was really nothing like a woman caught in the throes of lovemaking! Somehow, having just seen Yvette in that condition made Carruthers long the more to see Dora in that same flustered, impassioned state. Before today, he might have doubted that she could allow herself to feel. He had thought than an innocent lady, long settled into a celibate role, would need weeks, months perhaps, of tender soothing. But she had been so fiery, so lively in her anger and outrage! It remained only to turn that same energy onto love.

By the time Carruthers turned into Mount Street, he was eagerly awaiting the coming day. He'd go to Jackson's first thing in the morning and spar with the master. That, followed by a cold bath, should calm him down.

DORA PROMISED HERSELF she would say nothing to anyone of the many disasters that had befallen her at Ashvale. Still, it was not more than a day after that fateful excursion that she was calling upon Amelia Lavenham, the only person in London she trusted as a friend.

Amelia provided tea and a sympathetic ear over a private interview in her small saloon. "My heavens," she was soon exclaiming, "what a day you must have had! Oh, to have been there. Now—" she counted on her fingers "—one: Sir James Perry proposes. Two: Carruthers offers you a *carte blanche*. And three: you find that Carruthers has seduced your little cousin. My dear girl, it passes all belief. Now, are you certain of what happened?" Seeing Dora's vexed expression, Amelia held back the laugh that had almost escaped her.

"Certainly," Dora was retorting. "Sir James—"

Amelia waved her hand. "Oh, I didn't mean I doubted that prosy old thing wants to marry you. Pity you didn't dash his hopes more effectively, but I assure you it would have taken a kick in the teeth to get through to the man. From what I've seen of him, he's always been oblivious to anything but his own consequence. No, it's the other things. Carruthers. How has he turned out to be such a villain?"

Dora scowled. Much as she longed to, she simply couldn't betray the solemn oath she had made to that poor creature, Yvette, that she would never mention how the two of them had spoken of Carruthers. She confined herself to saying simply, "The man's a horrid libertine. I wouldn't put anything past him, but it still defies belief that he seduced Augusta Bracken."

"And you are certain he did?"

"He didn't deny it when I accused him," Dora said, reddening as she remembered that interview. And kissing her on the heels of his promise to publish notice of his marriage with Augusta! "And she was absolutely aghast that I'd walked in on them. Oh, her guilt was obvious, the poor misguided little soul. She has been avoiding me ever since, you know, she's so ashamed of herself. But at least he's willing to make amends to the girl. I doubt very much that they will suit, but they certainly must marry now with such a thing between them."

Amelia shook her head. "I can't see that child as a loose woman. You simply must have heard wrong," she insisted. "Think back. What did the two of them say?"

Dora had forgotten the original words, but she retained a vivid general impression of the conversation she had so improperly overheard. "She was worried over keeping such a shocking secret. He assured her she'd done nothing wrong, that she'd only acted out of love. Love, if you please! When not an hour before he had been mauling me about as though I were a— As though I were what he wants me to be. The wretched man! He must have been out of his mind to take advantage of her."

"Of her," repeated Amelia with a keen look at Dora's flushed face and snapping eyes.

"And I have to be glad, for Augusta's sake, that Carruthers agreed to marry her," Dora went on. Her voice was trembling slightly. "It would have killed me to have to inform Sir Giles of this. I may still have to, you know, if that marriage notice doesn't appear within the time I've set out."

"You certainly were diligent in that regard, my dear," said Amelia. "Where does Augusta's Mr. Farley enter into all this?"

"He doesn't," Dora said with a shake of her head. "They were thrown together once or twice during the day, to be sure, but Augusta is such an adept at playacting. I couldn't catch a hint in her manner toward him of any of the fondness she used to swear to. Oh, dear." Thoughts of Edgar Farley's plight caused a tear to roll out of her eye, and she brushed it away with an apologetic smile. "Poor young man. Even if Carruthers should cry off—and I wouldn't put it past him—Farley couldn't possibly marry Augusta now that she's been ruined by another."

"Well, no." Briskly Amelia poured some more tea and passed comfit cakes. "Did it ever occur to you, dear, that Augusta and Mr. Farley might be hiding their affection for one another, since they were in front of her parents?"

"No," said Dora. "I have thought of that possibility, but now with this revelation about Augusta and Carruthers I can't see how—"

Amelia looked at her friend keenly and changed the subject. "Now, let me hear some more about your plan to snag Miss Farley for Sir James Perry. I'll have to think about the Carruthers problem, my dear. It's so very curious. He's always been the soul of honour, whatever his little interests."

Dora was round-eyed at her friend's lack of concern about the seduction of an innocent young lady. She attributed it to the sophistication that came of years in the ton. Putting Carruthers out of her own mind with a determined effort, she detailed to Amelia her schemes for setting Selina Farley in Sir James's way. "I somehow know I'll have the aid of old Mrs. Farley, so it shouldn't be too difficult."

Her companion merely nodded. She was absorbed in her own plan to speak with Lawrence Carruthers as soon as could be. She quite longed to hear his version of these happenings.

Amelia glanced over at her friend. Dora had never looked prettier—sure sign of a woman in love. It would be so delightful to see her settled at last! Could her wild story have even the germ of truth? Or was it merely that so many years as a spinster had finally led poor Dora to start imagining offers, illicit or otherwise, where none existed? Amelia had heard of this phenomenon, but she had never imagined such a thing happening to a friend of one's own; and moreover someone of the same age as oneself.

CHAPTER FOURTEEN

AMELIA LAVENHAM GOT RIGHT DOWN to business. As soon as Dora left her house she wrote a short note to Mr. Carruthers, in which she promised him that he would learn something much to his advantage if he would but visit her later in the day. To her delight, Lawrence Carruthers actually appeared in her drawing room at the appointed time.

"Oh, sir, how good of you to answer my little summons." Amelia moved gracefully across the room, her hand outstretched. She dimpled in pleasure as Carruthers kissed it, then invited him to sit down in the chair opposite her own. There were already cordials set out on a nearby table; Amelia disliked being interrupted by servants during a private conference. Settling herself, she took up her needlework.

"Tiny garments, my lady?" asked Carruthers with a smile.

Amelia coloured prettily. "How clever of you, sir. Not one man in a thousand would have noticed what I was working on." She shook out the little infant dress she had been embroidering in her own clumsy, but painstaking, style. "We haven't announced it yet, mind you, but my little boy expects a playmate sometime in the fall."

"I'm delighted for you, ma'am."

It occurred to Amelia that she hadn't even told Dora this news and that her friend must have been preoccupied indeed not to have questioned her on the matter. Amelia had been working on the same small white dress when she had visited with Dora earlier in the day, and the dear girl's eyes were usually so sharp.

Accepting Carruthers's congratulations with a smile and an adjuration not to bruit the news about as yet, Amelia approached the real reason for his summons. "I received a visit from my friend Miss Thornfield this morning," she began.

Carruthers leaned back in his chair, the picture of unconcern. But his attractive hazel eyes were glittering in amusement. "Miss Thornfield? And you thought I would be interested in news of your visitor?"

"I was certain you'd be most interested, sir," Amelia stated, looking wise. "I have eyes in my head, you know, and one would have to be dull indeed not to have noticed your attentions to my dear friend in these past weeks."

"Then my secret is out." Carruthers seemed to be rather pleased than not. "It would indeed be…interesting to hear what the lady said of me. I assume the two of you are confidantes? Old school friends, and all that?"

"She did take me into her confidence," Amelia admitted, her eyes twinkling.

"I see. I'd imagine the lady had a great deal to say to you on the subject of a certain libertine gentleman—if she any longer honours me with that title, which I doubt."

"I was quite shocked, sir!"

"As was I. Do you know the whole of it, milady? That besides offending Miss Thornfield mightily with my—how did she put it?—lewd designs, I've found myself bound to take Miss Augusta Bracken as my affianced wife before the week is out?"

Amelia joined the gentleman in a hearty laugh. "You can't think what a difficulty I had in keeping my countenance, Carruthers. And then, when Dora told me of Sir James Perry's proposal—''

This was news to Carruthers. He sat up straight. "What? That sly old fox. I might have known he'd wangled his way into my party for some such reason, but I had no idea he'd attempted the proposal." A sudden fear showed in his eyes. "She didn't accept him, did she?"

Amelia wasn't above teasing a charming man who was a bit too sure of himself. "Why, Sir James would be a very suitable match for Dora. All those children, and an establishment of her own. I wouldn't blame her if she did take him up on what I understand was a very flattering offer."

Carruthers's look of dismay was too pitiable, and too flattering to Dora, for Amelia to keep up the pretence for long. "She did refuse him, as it happens, and though he wouldn't really take no for an answer, Dora has a plan to get his mind off the match. I believe it involves your own cousin, sir. Miss Farley."

Frowning, Carruthers said, "Selina shouldn't be pushed into any such thing. I know she's had a hard time of it, stuck out in the country with her mother, not to mention a young brother, and I've lately discovered that the Farleys haven't been in easy circumstances. But I've planned to remedy that, you know, Lady Lavenham. With the boy provided for, I'm setting up an annuity for the womenfolk, and Selina won't have to marry against her inclinations."

"But if she should want to marry Sir James?"

Amelia's question hung in the air for a moment, and Carruthers's face betrayed the thought that no rational creature could harbour such a wish toward the unhappy baronet.

"Well, she could, you know," Amelia informed the gentleman, smiling into his transparent countenance. "But from what I hear of her, she won't let herself be drawn into anything she doesn't wish.''

''Cousin Selina can take care of herself,'' Carruthers agreed. ''Now tell me, my lady, how I'm to handle this situation with your opinionated schoolfellow?''

''For one thing, you might refrain from seducing her relations.''

''My lady, you can't seriously believe...''

Of course Amelia did not, but she demanded a full explanation, which, to her vexation, Carruthers couldn't give, saying the matter was not his secret. But he made up for this lack of openness by giving Lady Lavenham a heavily edited version of his night's adventure in Charles Street, ending with the very interesting revelation which he and a few guineas had been able to worm out of Farnham, Yvette's mostly loyal butler.

DORA WAS MEANWHILE wasting no time in her plan to bestow elsewhere the chubby hand of Sir James Perry, baronet. On returning from her visit with Amelia, she was summoned to Lady Bracken's side in the morning room.

''I've permitted dear Sir James to take you driving this afternoon, cousin, at five o'clock,'' that lady informed her with a meaning smile. ''When the poor man called while you were gone, he looked so disappointed over having missed you that I couldn't resist his plea, though I don't really consider it, uh, *convenable* for my companion to spend so much time away from me. After all...''

''Yes, Cousin Maud, the entire purpose of having a companion is defeated,'' Dora responded. ''I'd be happy to give up the drive. It would really distress me to neglect my duties. Why don't I send round a note to Sir James now declining the invitation? And is there anything I can do for you? Would you like a shawl, or shall I fetch your embroidery or your writing desk?''

These attempts to distract Lady Bracken were to no avail. "I can't have you disappoint Sir James," she said with playful insistence, "for he intimated that there was something very particular he wanted to say to you. Your indisposition yesterday made him delay the moment, but you mustn't worry, Cousin. He does have marriage in mind, and I plan to give your romance all the assistance I can. Oh, and while you're upstairs taking your bonnet off you might just bring me that copy of the *Ladies' Magazine* you'll find on my bed table. Ah, so kind.''

Dora was frowning as she went upstairs. Then inspiration struck her, and she flew to her own writing table, where she penned a very succinct note and sent it off to Mount Street by the two-penny post.

SIR JAMES WAS NOT COW-HANDED, Dora observed critically some hours later, but certainly he would never be asked into the Four In Hand Club. His gloved hands were heavy on the ribbons of the passable pair of greys, as he and Dora perched, both of them somewhat gingerly, upon the seat of a very high phaeton which Sir James had borrowed for the occasion from a friend. "It's been a long time since I took a lady driving," he confided to his fair companion as they tooled about the crowded carriage road in Hyde Park.

Dora, knowing that Sir James lacked imagination, had expected that he would choose the Park for their drive, and had he not done so, she had been prepared to tease him into it with a wheedling tale of how she loved to see society on promenade. She was glad that such a small subterfuge had been unnecessary, for she was saving all her slyness for the great events to come.

The intense concentration required to drive a high-perch phaeton for the first time was a stroke of luck for Dora. Sir James hadn't been able to seize a moment away from his task to regale her with another declaration. He hadn't even started in on a string of empty compliments she had grown to recognize as the prelude to a tender scene, so busy had the horses kept him. Now if only they would come upon the Farleys before long; for Dora wouldn't put it past Sir James to pull up under some tree and make again the dreaded offer of marriage. His manners today, despite his necessary preoccupation with the phaeton, left no doubt that he had totally disregarded the fact she had refused him the day before.

Dora let her eyes sweep the surrounding crowds, desperate to see the faces she wished to find. And suddenly she gave a start; for there, approaching on the other side of the carriage path, in an open tilbury surrounded by admiring gentlemen both on foot and on horseback, rode Yvette. Did the flashing dark eyes meet Dora's for just an instant in recognition, or was it only Dora's imagination?

How beautiful she was, thought Dora, sighing a little over the Cyprian's sumptuous pelisse and Parisian bonnet. How sophisticated as she flirts expertly with all those men. Against her will, Dora envisioned that beauty and charm in the arms of Lawrence Carruthers, where she herself had been the day before. Her face crimsoned at the very thought. And that bruise that Yvette had shown her. Had it been inflicted in anger, as the courtesan had intimated, or in passion? Dora stared at Yvette, transfixed with the shock of her new thought.

"Miss Thornfield, *that* is not a woman you should notice." The rasping voice of Sir James Perry brought her out of her revery. "Please! Avert your eyes, ma'am. That is a notorious woman of the town."

Dora obediently turned her eyes to her companion, who had bristled up in indignation presumably at the very thought of a woman of that sort. "Forgive me, Sir James, I had no idea," she replied in her most demure style, lowering her lashes.

Sir James beamed. "Ah, so modest, so innocent. Dear Miss Thornfield, do allow me to manoeuvre these resty animals to a more secluded spot—perhaps over there by the water—and we shall continue with the talk that your illness yesterday so unfortunately interrupted. My daughters are most anxious..."

Wondering how a refusal of his suit had ever transformed itself in this gentleman's mind into an interrupted talk, Dora steeled herself for the coming ordeal. The Park was so crowded, it was no wonder she hadn't been able to find the persons she sought.

"Miss Thornfield!"

Dora whirled about on the narrow seat, clutching at the small armrest and teetering a little. "Why, Sir James, it's Mrs. Farley and her daughter. Oh, Mrs. Farley, what a nice surprise."

The older lady, grim and determined in her serviceable old walking boots, approached the phaeton, propelling her daughter before her. She betrayed no sign that this meeting had been prearranged. It was obvious from the honest surprise and pleasure bedecking Selina Farley's face that her mother had not divulged the scheme to her.

Sir James bowed as best he could from his unsteady seat, and it occurred to Dora that here was a problem she had not prepared for. Sir James had left his groom behind, probably because he didn't want to propose under the eye of a servant, and it was thus impossible for him to take Selina Farley up with him, as Dora had planned. Sir James couldn't leave the horses, and there was no one else to help Dora down, and Miss Farley up.

These vexatious thoughts flashed through Dora's mind in an instant, and she determined to make the most of the meeting regardless. "What a pleasant outing we had yesterday," she began.

Mrs. Farley murmured some agreement, but her daughter was more vocal. "Oh, indeed it was delightful to see Cousin Lawrence's country seat. And, Sir James, I must tell you how pleased I was to make the acquaintance of your sweet daughters. They so entertained me on the ride back to London."

A flirtatious intent was just barely discernible, and Dora realized that the practical Selina was indeed making a push to secure her future. And considering what her past must have been, pinching pennies in the country, who could blame her? Dora knew from Augusta's stories that the Farleys had made do for years on only the widowed Mrs. Farley's small jointure; and the expense of sending the young man to university would have plunged his womenfolk even deeper into the genteel shabbiness that was revealed today in their simple, much used walking costumes.

Sir James was revelling in the unaccustomed delight of being surrounded by women. "Ah, dear Miss Farley, Caroline and Alice were quite as pleased with you. Shall I convey your greetings to them?" He threw a sidelong glance Miss Thornfield's way, and she was encouraged by its furtive aspect. Sir James had become a man with two entanglements! How diverting.

Miss Farley coyly congratulated Miss Thornfield for having the courage to ride in such a high vehicle.

"Oh, it's nothing. You ought to try it yourself," Dora answered airily.

"Oh! I've never ridden in anything more sporting than my brother's gig," protested Miss Farley.

"Dear ma'am, it would be my pleasure to convey you sometime," Sir James put in, his words a little unsteady since he was in the process of trying to control the restive greys.

"And what better time than the present?" chimed in a male voice that Dora knew only too well. Mr. Carruthers stepped up to the group, appearing out of the crowd of pedestrians as if by magic. "Dear Miss Thornfield! And Cousin Olivia and Cousin Selina! I'd hoped to catch up with you. The servants told me you'd gone walking."

"The Park at the fashionable hour has been recommended to us as one of the sights of town," Mrs. Farley said with a pleasant nod to her cousin.

"Has it?" Mr. Carruthers's eyes flickered over Dora for an instant, and he smiled at the cold, repressive expression that now bedecked her charming face. Then he turned to Sir James. "Sir, a pleasure to meet you here. I couldn't help overhearing. Why don't you take Cousin Selina on a turn about the Park while I wait with the other ladies? I'll wager she'd love to tell her friends back home she'd driven in a sporting vehicle with a London buck."

Unfortunately she would only be able to say she'd taken a shaky turn around the Park with a boring widower, was Dora's unworthy thought as she forced herself to greet Mr. Carruthers pleasantly and urge Miss Farley to trade places with herself. How unfortunate that Carruthers had happened by, but he did have his use at the moment. He could help Selina up, and—dear heaven—he would help *her* down.

Sir James, puffed up at the thought of himself as a London buck, asked Miss Thornfield if she would mind standing about for a few minutes, or if they should endeavour to fit three?

"Oh, you would be much too crowded. I'm sure it would frighten both ladies," said Mr. Carruthers. "Miss Thornfield, may I?" And before she had steeled herself for such a disaster, Dora found herself being lifted down from the phaeton. Carruthers's hands were tight and possessive, yet somehow seemed to caress her gently as he jumped her down. When she landed safely on the ground, those same strong hands retained their hold around her waist for an instant too long, and she dared a glance up into his hazel eyes. She quickly directed her attention to the ground. His look was as caressing as his hands had been.

The man was so maddening, so sure of himself, after all that had happened yesterday! Dora was fuming while Carruthers assisted his cousin Selina up into the phaeton.

"Do be careful, dear," put in Mrs. Farley. She looked up at the high, fragile carriage in real concern now that her daughter was actually in it.

"Mama, you worry too much," said Selina with an uncharacteristic tinkling laugh, and the phaeton moved away.

Carruthers took Miss Thornfield's arm and Mrs. Farley's, and began a slow promenade suitable to the elderly lady's needs. "Well, ladies, what do you think? Will those two make a match of it?"

"Cousin! My Selina met the man only yesterday," protested Mrs. Farley. "And she is far beyond the age of hanging out for a husband."

"Still, he is a very respectable man, and in great need of a wife," Carruthers persisted. "Wouldn't you say so, Miss Thornfield?"

Dora had the uneasy feeling that Carruthers knew all about Sir James's proposal to her yesterday. She could feel him teasing her with every word. "I can't presume to know the needs of another person, sir," she answered.

"Ah, ladies, both of you so reticent," sighed Carruthers. "Why not simply admit that you've thrown Selina into the arms of our worthy baronet? It's to be hoped she won't let herself be caught in anything objectionable."

Mrs. Farley finally gave over and laughed with her cousin. "Lawrence, you're not to tease poor Selina over this. Miss Thornfield and I might think this match a good thing, but it will be up to Selina when all is said and done. And have no fear that marriage to a "worthy baronet" would be one whit more objectionable than a youth wasted in the depths of Surrey at the beck and call of a crab-cross old mother and a lively young brother."

The lady spoke with sincerity, her voice shaking a little over the last words, and Dora was touched. "Your daughter would never agree with your estimation of her life, ma'am," she felt compelled to say. "I can see how fond she is of you and her brother."

"I can second that," added Carruthers. "You a crab-cross old mother, Cousin Olivia? Never." And, giving his cousin no chance to brood further on her daughter's misspent years, he initiated a flood of teasing talk that kept both of his companions cheerfully entertained.

At least Dora, bound as if by leather thongs to one of his arms, had to pretend to be comfortable. Not for anything would she have revealed her hatred of this man in front of Mrs. Farley. But, oh, how she longed to send at least one or two barbed comments his way. And what was he doing lounging about the Park in the first place? He ought to be at the side of poor Augusta. The child hadn't emerged from her chamber all day. She was probably prostrate with shame that her ruin had been discovered, and where was her seducer? Not comforting her, nor assuring his young victim that he would make an honest woman of her, but chatting and laughing as though he hadn't a care in the world, and one of the women on his arm the very one he had deigned as his next ladybird!

But manners demanded that Miss Thornfield, Mr. Carruthers, and Mrs. Farley stroll about in complete charity, and so they did. When the phaeton returned and was drawn to a shaky halt before the trio, Carruthers assisted his cousin Selina down and returned Dora to the perch beside Sir James. Carruthers's arms were no less intimate the second time he held Miss Thornfield's rigid figure, and she had to practise breathing deeply in order to avoid disgracing herself forever by melting into the embrace of the vile seducer.

When she and Sir James were alone, her escort said with a cough, "Well, what say I take you home now, ma'am? It's growing late."

Dora realized that he was not going to repeat his offer of marriage; thus she couldn't resist goading him a little. "But, sir, didn't you have something to ask me?" There was a plaintive note in her voice.

A louder cough from her middle-aged suitor. "Why, yes, ma'am, there was. I was simply going to urge you to maintain our friendship, despite my, er, hasty words to you yesterday."

It was with difficulty that Dora restrained herself from sending up a cheer to Selina Farley. Assuring the baronet of her eternal friendship, she smiled all the way home.

CHAPTER FIFTEEN

DORA HAD BEEN TRYING to speak to Augusta all day. When she returned from her drive with Sir James in the Park, it was time to dress for dinner. Dora judged that the only place her young quarry would be was in her bed chamber under the ministrations of her mama's dresser, who always "did" the daughter of the house first before undertaking the more complex chore of readying her ladyship for public scrutiny.

Dora knocked on the door of Augusta's room in the certainty that this wouldn't be taken as a sign that anything was amiss. It was no uncommon thing for the cousins to visit one another's chambers while dressing for the evening, though more often it would be Augusta who would burst into Dora's small sanctum, wanting advice about a ribbon or a quite impossible headdress of plumes.

Meeker, Lady Bracken's haughty tiring-woman, opened the door.

"I'd like to talk to my cousin," Dora said pleasantly, starting forward.

But the woman didn't stand aside. "Ma'am, Miss Bracken is...engaged," she said with a very expressive shrug of the shoulders.

Dora could only nod and go on her way down the hall, wondering how Augusta would manage to avoid her for the entire evening. It was most important that she and the girl converse before long, for not only did Augusta stand in need of more reassurance that her secret was safe—this was obvious from her hole-in-corner manner!—but Dora needed to hear, from Augusta's own lips, exactly how far her intrigue with Carruthers had gone.

In this spirit of imminent discovery, Dora got into the first evening gown to hand, gave her hair a quick brush, put on a fresh lace evening cap and went down to the drawing room, for if she were first into the room she could certainly pounce on Augusta.

"Well! Greaves said some of the family would be down shortly, but I never expected him to grant me a tête-à-tête with the lady of my heart," said Mr. Carruthers, crossing the room with his hand outstretched. He had been standing by the window, and the last rays of the evening sun illuminated his figure in the moment before he stepped out of the light.

Dora could hardly refuse the hand, and irritated at her own vanity, she regretted her lack of primping. She shook the hand firmly but dismissively, not meeting the gentleman's eyes.

"You know, much as I deplore the wearing of caps in young women of your time of life, I must admit that confection is very becoming," said Carruthers, enjoying the sight of the blonde curls and white lace. So might she look in a boudoir cap...

Dora looked away, seething. Her heart had lifted at his compliment. This was an impossible situation.

"Aren't you going to ask me how I have the gall to show my face in the bosom of the family I've disgraced?" enquired Carruthers.

Sighing over his good-humoured, insolent smile, Dora again declined to answer. Instead she bowed, stepped past the gentleman and took an isolated seat in one corner of the room: her habitual chair. In fact, her work-bag was sitting

on the table next to it, and she proceeded to extract the bit
of embroidery from it.

"What fine work you do, ma'am," said Carruthers. Un-
daunted by the lady's frozen manner, he drew up a hard
chair to sit near her. "Don't get up, please," he added.
"Think how it would look if some of the others were to
come in to find me chasing you round the room."

Dora looked up, her grey eyes blazing. "You are insufferable," she hissed. "How on earth could you be so bold?
Little Augusta is already avoiding me like the plague since
yesterday's revelations. What could you be thinking of?
She'll surely die of shame if she's obliged to sit down to
dinner with you. Unless—" she hesitated, searching his face
with an odd sensation of hope mixed with dread "—you've
settled things with Sir Giles, and the marriage is arranged?"

"Not quite that. You're precipitate, ma'am," Carruthers
responded affably. "May I remind you that you gave me one
week to organize that matter?"

"Then why are you putting the child through this torture?"

"The child?" echoed Carruthers with a knowing smile.
Dora realized that her last words had been strident, and
frowned. An inconvenient memory of Carruthers's arms
around her that afternoon as he'd lifted her down from Sir
James's phaeton was assailing her mind at the moment and
making her feel quite the injured party. She wanted to be in
his arms right now! Now, when she knew him for a villain.
Only a cad would try to elicit a sensual response from a
woman who had refused his advances. For he must be trying
to tease her into confusion; such feelings as were running
through her could never arise unprovoked.

"If you must know, Lady Bracken insisted that I and my
houseguests join your charming group this evening," said

Carruthers. "I'll admit to you that it wasn't easy to get her to include the Farleys."

"And where are they?" Dora demanded, casting her eyes round the drawing room. Yes, it was empty, thank goodness. What she and Carruthers were having at the moment was much too near an unpleasant scene for it to be witnessed by others.

"Young Edgar is bringing the ladies. I didn't realize until we'd returned from the Park that I hadn't mentioned this dinner to them, and they needed a little time to prepare. I came on ahead, hoping to have speech with either you or Miss Bracken before the general gathering began. Rude of me to appear early, would you say?"

"You rude, Mr. Carruthers? Say, rather, unscrupulous, libertine and absolutely shameless. That poor young man, your cousin! Don't you feel it a bit cruel to put him and Augusta in company for an evening, considering how things stand?"

Carruthers shrugged. "I thought it would be a good idea. Now on to the subject of our talk, Miss Thornfield." He hesitated, giving her one of those intimate looks which seemed to penetrate not only to her undergarments but all the way to her heart. "You won't allow me to call you Dora, as I would wish?"

"Certainly not," snapped the lady. "And we have nothing to talk about, sir."

"*Au contraire, mademoiselle*, as a former associate of mine would have said," Carruthers replied. "I've many questions to ask you regarding your behaviour. It's come to my attention that you, Miss Thornfield, have been engaging in some altogether questionable activities of late."

Wondering what he meant, Dora said, "Nothing so questionable as what you yourself have asked me to do, sir. Now please leave me alone. It's occurred to me that it's improper for us to be sitting by ourselves, and I must run upstairs again and wait for the ladies.'' She rose, inching past her tormenter, whose broad shoulder shifted to one side, but she couldn't avoid brushing his leg as she moved to safety. Even that slight touch burned Dora in her present mood. A low, sensuous chuckle followed her as, cheeks red, she stalked to the door.

It opened before she could get there, and Lady Bracken stood on the threshold. "Cousin Theodora! What is the meaning of this? I know you're hardly of an age to need a chaperone, but even so, to sit alone with a gentleman! Ah, Mr. Carruthers.'' Lady Bracken moved forward with a welcoming smile. Her first words had been uttered in an angry hiss, but her greeting to Carruthers was graciousness itself.

The gentleman rose and responded with thanks for the invitation. "The rest of my party will be along soon, my lady. You'll forgive your cousin and me for our shocking lapse? Poor Miss Thornfield walked in on me unawares, and I gave her no chance for escape.''

"Oh, sir, naturally you couldn't help who walked into the room," gushed Lady Bracken, motioning Carruthers to a place next to her on the sofa. Dora she studiously ignored, and as the room was now well tenanted, her ladyship's companion felt safe in returning to the chair where her embroidery still lay. "Now where is my daughter?" Lady Bracken went on with an arch look at Carruthers. "She was so excited, sir, that you would be dining with us this evening—the very least we could do, by the way, to repay you for that charming excursion to Ashvale. All of us enjoyed it so much, but especially my Augusta. Ah, Cousin—" she raised her voice and turned to where Dora sat, pretending to outline a rose on the purse she was working "—I'm a terribly absentminded creature. How did your outing with Sir James go? Do you have some news for us, perhaps?"

"Good heavens no, Cousin Maud," Dora returned a little snappishly. Out of the corner of her eye she could see that
Mr. Carruthers looked most amused by this turn in the
conversation.

Lady Bracken's goading blessedly came to an end when
Sir Giles entered. The burst of greetings and masculine
asides which then ensued were halted only by Greaves, who
announced the Farley party.

The three from Surrey, looking as countrified and out of
place as ever, and for this reason more appealing, were ushered into the room. Edgar, escorting his womenfolk, looked
flushed and happy, Dora noted in surprise; not at all the
mood one would expect from a young man who was being
forced to spend the evening gazing from afar on the girl who
used to love him.

As for Mrs. Farley, she bore her hostess's cold civilities
for a few moments, told Cousin Carruthers that she didn't
care for the chair he had placed for her so near the fire and
approached Miss Thornfield.

"What a pretty piece of work, my dear," she said loudly,
taking the chair next to Dora's. Then, leaning forward, she
said softly, "We've done it, Miss Thornfield. When he had
her in the phaeton today, he asked if he might call."

"What wonderful news," replied Dora in as soft a voice,
knowing very well who the "he" in question was. A glance
at Selina Farley, talking to her brother and Carruthers
across the room, revealed no signs of depression on the features of that long-suffering spinster. She looked quite happy
on the contrary, more animated than Dora remembered
seeing her.

Dora and Mrs. Farley smiled at each other in triumph.

"Both my children settled so happily," Mrs. Farley said
with a sigh. "Not but what it's a bit premature to talk of

Selina as being settled. But from what I hear of Sir James Perry, my dear, I can't but have every hope."

"Did you say both your children settled?" Dora queried.

"Why..." Mrs. Farley hesitated, and the pleasant face under the widow's cap looked almost furtive. "I'm letting myself run on in my excitement at Selina's beau. Do forgive me, Miss Thornfield. It's a question of a family confidence...."

"Oh, to be sure," Dora answered, mystified, but assuming that Mrs. Farley was only referring to some possibility of patronage for her son. Perhaps she feared bad luck if she spoke too soon!

Lady Bracken swept across the room. "Ah, are you entertaining Mrs. Farley, Cousin Theodora? How good of you. Now do be a lamb and run up to my Augusta's chamber. I don't know what could be keeping the sweet child, but dinner will be served in a very few minutes and she must be here. Mr. Carruthers is to hand her in."

"I'll go at once." And Dora, hoping that Augusta wouldn't hide in the wardrobe on finding out who it was come to fetch her, obligingly went upstairs.

There was no answer to her scratch at the bed-chamber door. "Augusta!" she called. "May I come in?" She opened the door, rattling the handle a little as a kind of warning in case the child did want to hide in the wardrobe or under the bed.

At first glance the beruffled bed chamber appeared to be empty. "Augusta?" ventured Dora, stepping forward. On impulse she drew aside the pink curtains of the bed, and there was revealed a sad little figure in white mousseline de soie. "My dear, you wouldn't want them to have to wait dinner, would you?"

Augusta turned large, woeful eyes on her cousin. "Oh, how can I possibly go down? Whyever did Mama send you? Oh, Cousin, I'm so very, very ashamed."

Dora sat down on the bed and put her arms around the young girl. No stern lectures were warranted here. "It will be all right, dear, I promise you. Mr. Carruthers has sworn—"

"He's been too good to me," said Augusta with a disheartened sigh. "But how was I to know that you would consider it such an enormity?"

"Why, Augusta, I believe everyone would think as I do," Dora responded in surprise. The chit's moral education had been sadly neglected if she could even doubt that ruining herself was anything but an enormity. Well, such frivolous lack of thought was only to be expected from Cousin Maud.

Augusta said quaveringly, "Then if anyone ever found out what I'd done—"

"Oh, child, you must never tell anyone," exclaimed Dora. "And if you marry soon enough, any, er, mistake that may have happened will make no difference. By the way," said Dora, deciding to satisfy her curiosity on a certain point, "has this been going on for long?"

"Weeks," Augusta admitted, with a sidelong look at her cousin's face.

"Good Lord! That dreadful man," gasped Dora, hugging the girl even tighter to her. "Have you noticed any, well, ill effects yet, my dear?"

"What in the world are you talking about, Dora?" Augusta asked, true mystification in her eyes.

Dora conceded that it was just barely possible for a young creature to have indulged in amorous exploits without considering the danger of getting with child; and, as the damage could well be done, she didn't want to draw Augusta's attention to it now. She would make certain, though, that the marriage came off as soon as could be. Weeks, indeed. And Carruthers had just said, down in the drawing room, that he wasn't quite ready to ask for Augusta's hand. The swine!

Before Dora could think of a way to phrase some remark to replace her intended question about a pregnancy, there was a scratch at the door, for which interruption the older of the cousins was most grateful. Woman-to-woman talks were difficult things! The intruder proved to be a footman, bearing the message that dinner was on table.

"Heavens," said Dora, waving Silas away with thanks, "I'd forgotten dinner. You must go down, child. And don't worry. I don't blame you for what happened. It was hardly your fault. How could you stand up to an experienced rake?"

Augusta, engaged in smoothing her dress and pinching her pale cheeks, stared at Dora in surprise. "An experienced rake?" she repeated blankly.

"Oh, never mind, he's probably presented himself to you as quite the misunderstood pillar of virtue," Dora responded a touch impatiently. Really, it was too much for a ruined girl to be so blind about her seducer! But there was no time to rectify the matter now.

"Well, I'm glad you don't think it my fault. I've been ever so afraid to see you since you... Since yesterday at Ashvale," Augusta said, as the cousins moved quickly down to the drawing room. "Can we truly be friends again, Dora?"

"My dearest, we'll always be friends," Dora assured the young girl with the best smile she could muster, and they were able to join the others with a tolerable ease of manner between them.

Dinner was, for Dora, a supreme exercise in patience. Lady Bracken had invited Captain Laughton and his rich, elderly uncle, General Sir Percival Laughton, to make the numbers even, and it was the crusty general rather than his handsome nephew who was placed next to Dora. Sir Percival, who was rather deaf and quite nearsighted, did not challenge Dora's conversational powers overmuch, for he obviously preferred his dinner to female companionship, even though Mrs. Farley, on his other side, did her best to lure him with questions about his gout.

Dora was glad that Sir Percival's "infirmity"—that well-known tendency to make advances to women when he was in liquor—hadn't surfaced tonight. How dreadful if he should pinch Mrs. Farley! The elderly lady was obviously unaware of his reputation.

Captain Laughton, between Augusta and Selina Farley, smiled at Dora across the table from time to time, and she managed to wrest one or two remarks from her other dinner partner, Edgar Farley, when that youth wasn't staring raptly at Augusta.

"Do you stay much longer in town, sir?" she asked the young clergyman.

"Yes, ma'am," he responded. "That is, I don't really know my mother's preference, but Cousin Carruthers has told us not to be in a hurry to leave. He's the best of men, Miss Thornfield." Mr. Farley's eyes shone with youthful admiration.

Dora's heart was heavy. If the young man only knew the foul deeds his adored cousin had been perpetrating lately! It was nearly impossible to listen to this innocent sing the praises of such a vile impostor, and she could swear that the perfidious Carruthers would merely be amused if he could know how thoroughly he had hoodwinked his relations. She stole a look across the table to where Carruthers, at Lady Bracken's right, was having a low-voiced conversation with Augusta on his other side. Happening to catch the man's

eye, Dora couldn't resist glaring at him, but received in return only a raking glance.

"Mr. Carruthers is an interesting sort of man," Dora
managed as a response, of sorts, to Edgar Farley's fulsome
praise.

The young man was quick to agree. "He's spared no
pains to see to it that our visit to town has lacked for nothing."

"I believe he's introduced you to influential men, in aid
of your career?" Dora ventured, remembering her curiosity about Mrs. Farley's remark that both her children were
to be settled.

"There was hardly any need for that, ma'am, but as it
happens he has taken me to see several well-placed men of
the cloth."

"No need? But aren't you looking for a living?" Dora
had got out the question before she remembered how rude
it was.

Luckily the young man was willing to overlook her lapse.
"I'm a clergyman, ma'am. Naturally I would be glad of
occupation," he said with an incline of his head. "But that
sort of thing takes care of itself, you know."

Wondering whether this was an allusion to the notion that
God will provide, or whether Mr. Farley was simply too naïf
for words, Dora nodded. Edgar's attention was called by his
sister then, and Dora had to go back to her plate, it being a
much more entertaining companion than General
Laughton.

THE GENERAL HAD BEEN such an oblivious dinner partner
that in spite of his rakish reputation Dora was astonished
when, upon the gentlemen joining the ladies later in the
evening, the elderly man made straight for her side. "You

seem a fine, spirited filly,'' Sir Percival began with a shocking leer, when his nephew rushed up behind him.

"Uncle, I believe Sir Giles was wanting to show you some
of his volumes on India. He's anxious to compare your
memory with that of Beatson on the war with the Tippoo
Sultan. He has a copy of Beatson's book. If you'd come
along?''

The general uttered something that sounded like
"Grmph," but he toddled away tamely enough on the arm
of Sir Giles, who had been a few steps behind the captain.

Sir Giles winked at Dora as he bore her newest spark away
with him, and she looked into the captain's eyes with barely
suppressed amusement. "How kind of you gentlemen.''

"The general started singing your praises over his second
bottle, so Sir Giles and I were forewarned," Laughton answered. "My uncle can be a handful. Be warned for the rest
of the evening, ma'am, and steer clear.''

"Captain Laughton!'' came the commanding voice of
Lady Bracken. "Perhaps you didn't hear what I said as you
sped past my chair. Augusta is about to begin playing, and
I know you favour harp music.''

Dora and her companion started like guilty lovers, and
chivalry demanded that the captain forthwith leave Miss
Thornfield's side to take a place near the harp, which Dora
had every reason to know Augusta had not studied to much
effect.

However, entertainment by young ladies was a common
purgatory at a small dinner party, and Dora resolved to follow the captain, though she wouldn't risk sitting near him
for the impromptu concert. How very nice that gentleman
was. Perhaps, in time, when the memory of Mr.
Carruthers's touch had faded somewhat, one might come to
be fond of such a pleasant and suitable man as Laughton.
Dora frowned, trying to imagine herself addressing him as

Thomas, allowing him to kiss her, to caress her in the manner that a certain other gentleman in the room had done.

"You seem embarrassed, Miss Thornfield," Mr. Carruthers said very near her ear. "I hope it isn't still on account of General Laughton's assault? A harmless gentleman, I assure you."

Dora whirled and found herself looking into the very face that had just, in her imaginings, been descending on hers for a passionate kiss. The attempt to replace Carruthers with Laughton in those fancies had been totally inefficacious. "I'd find a harmless gentleman quite restful, after my late experiences," she said in a deceptively mild voice.

"Indeed? Well, each to his own. Now I want to talk to you." Carruthers seized the lady's arm and led her a little way into the shadows at one end of the room. All other guests were engaged at the moment in mustering for the harp recital. "I'm happy to hear that one of your misconceptions is at an end. According to Miss Bracken, you've quite forgiven her little boldness, which she assures me you now know all about. Do you admit, ma'am, that you've wronged both myself and the young lady? And jumped to a ludicrous conclusion, I might add. But now that you do know all, as Miss Bracken phrases it, you and I can certainly begin anew."

Dora gasped. She hadn't resisted his taking her into semi-privacy for fear of causing a scene, but now she wrenched her arm free of his hand. "Mr. Carruthers, how dare you? I've told you before, and I now repeat, I will have nothing to do with the seducer of that poor young girl. You are to marry her—soon—and though our paths may cross, we can never be more than nodding acquaintances. Naturally I have assured poor Augusta of my eternal friendship and my help. She'll probably need it." And turning on her heel, Dora did not walk so much as flounce across the room, where she sat by the side of her employer for the rest of the evening, rising only to take over the duties of the tea tray and to fetch a shawl for Cousin Maud.

She ignored Carruthers's quizzical glances and didn't dignify with her attention a whispered conference the gentleman had with Augusta at the end of the party. She was fed to the teeth with second guessing that particular pair of clandestine lovers.

CHAPTER SIXTEEN

DORA'S REST WAS TORMENTED by dreams of Carruthers, who seemed to delight in teasing her newly awakened sensibilities even outside the everyday realm. She was furious at her would-be seducer by five o'clock in the morning, when she turned on her hot pillow for the ten thousandth time.

"Dora!" A whisper came from beyond the bed curtains, and Dora was startled into near consciousness.

Augusta's small, nightcapped head, lit by a candle, peeked through the curtains. "Oh, you're awake." She sighed in relief.

"In a manner of speaking," Dora mumbled, struggling to place an extra pillow behind her back as she sat up.

Augusta hastened to perform this office after setting her candle down on the bed table; then she plopped down on the simple woollen comforter, very bright-eyed for a normally lazy girl at such an unreasonably early hour.

"I simply couldn't wait," she announced. "Dora, Mr. Carruthers told me to give you all the details as soon as possible, and it's simply ages till breakfast."

Dora was still fighting her way out of the land of dreams. "Carruthers? Details?" she repeated. Then her eyes flew wide open. "Details of what, dear? I'm certain he didn't mean—"

"He insisted that you didn't yet know everything about...about what made you so angry at me," Augusta affirmed. She had the grace to look a little ashamed.

Dora was not certain that she was up to a confession of such magnitude. "Now, Augusta, no matter what Mr. Carruthers may instruct you to do, I'm certain he wouldn't mean for us both to be embarrassed," she said, though she was fairly sure that Mr. Carruthers would, in fact, derive considerable enjoyment from disconcerting *her*. And the past had already proven him to be far from sympathetic to Augusta's best interests.

"Well, he made me promise faithfully," Augusta responded. She set her small jaw in a good imitation of her mother at that lady's most determined.

Dora sighed and half closed her eyes, trying to brace herself for a detailed account of a maiden's fall from grace.

"It all started at the Vining ball, when we met Mr. Carruthers," Augusta began. "Though he often used to visit Papa, I had never been introduced, for I wasn't out yet. But I knew of him, since my Edgar is his heir."

"Your Edgar?" Dora interrupted. "My dear girl, you surely don't still harbour feelings of attachment to Mr. Farley?"

"Why, Dora," said Augusta, "Mr. Farley is the man I love."

This was too much, given the circumstances, and Dora could do no more than gape. She had thought that the new ideas on educating modern misses turned them into stodgy prigs. Augusta was beginning to sound like a female libertine!

Augusta rushed on. "And knowing how hopeless my marriage with Edgar was as things stood, I somehow found the courage to approach Mr. Carruthers at the ball, while we were dancing. I felt...Well, Dora, can't you agree that a rich man who is related to a young man who needs help is obligated to provide that help?''

"Well, in theory, of course." Dora was becoming very confused by this line of talk.

She was even more confused when Augusta leaned forward and gave her a hearty hug. "Oh, I knew you'd think so! Though, since naturally I had to keep the thing secret from Mama and Papa, I simply couldn't confide in you."

The thing! Dora could only shake her head and wonder if Augusta possessed any seriousness of mind at all. And what was this about a rich man helping a relation?

"Besides," Augusta said, "I've observed that from time to time, Cousin, you can be a little stiff."

"Stiff?" Dora sat up a bit straighter, for she recognized and had to agree with the criticism, though she didn't think it justified in this instance. "Stiff, because I would have disapproved of your ruin? Really, my dear."

Augusta gasped. "My ruin? Oh, Dora, even for a true prig, which I know you're not, that passes all bounds! You were upset when you found out, of course, for I did flout the proprieties. I'm well aware that begging Mr. Carruthers to do something for Edgar was overbold, but I never thought anyone would call it ruinous. Heavens! I'm proud of it!" She tossed her head as if in emphasis.

Her words had caused Dora to frown in bewilderment. "Augusta," she said slowly, "what we are discussing here—your relations with Mr. Carruthers—do you mean to tell me that all you've done is to ask Carruthers to help your young man?"

"Of course. How could I give up such a perfect chance to set dear Edgar on the road to prosperity? I had to seize the moment, Dora, for who could tell if Mr. Carruthers would ever ask me to dance again? Mr. Carruthers seemed so nice, too. I was sure he would need only a hint and something would be done for Edgar—and so it proved. And I've been deathly afraid ever since you found out that you'd tell Mama. I've even had to pretend that I didn't care for Edgar, just to be on the safe side. Mama would never let me hear the end of it if she knew that it was all on account of my meddling that Edgar has the means to marry me now."

"He does?"

"Yes." Augusta sighed, and a sunny smile broke out on her face. "Dear, sweet Mr. Carruthers has given the living of Ashvale to Edgar. Oh, didn't you think it a charming place when we went there the other day? It brings in quite a good income, too, and there will be plenty for me to do with refurnishing the vicarage, for Mr. Carruthers promised to fit it up for us as a wedding present."

Dora, staring unseeingly into the bed curtains, stopped listening. Augusta prattled on and on about Carruthers's kindness, and her cousin felt an urge to break into hysterical laughter. He hadn't seduced Augusta! That was all she could think of. Augusta's conversation with Carruthers the other day made perfect sense in this new connection. "You were motivated out of love," he had said to quieten the young girl's fears that she'd done something quite improper. Yes, it made sense. Oh, what a great relief—for the child's sake, of course.

"How very brave of you, Augusta, to collar a strange man and demand that he help your Edgar. I'm all admiration," she interjected into the middle of Augusta's raptures over Mr. Carruthers.

"Why, thank you, Dora," replied the girl with a surprised glance. Her starchy cousin was finally coming to understand why she'd had to do such a shocking thing. Mr. Carruthers had assured Augusta that Dora would understand, but remembering her cousin's wrath when she had first found out about it, Augusta had doubted very much that she would ever have the stern and proper lady's approval.

"If I'd known, I certainly wouldn't have betrayed you to your parents," Dora added. And she wouldn't have accused Carruthers of seducing the child, nor demanded that he marry her. He had doubtless spent the previous days in laughing at Dora's stupidity.

"Good, because I must swear you to secrecy now, besides," Augusta said. "If Mama or Papa ever should find out... Well, Papa would probably laugh, but Mama would have fits. When Edgar comes to ask for my hand, as we plan for him to do later on today, they must know only that Mr. Carruthers has *happened* to give him the living. And it's quite natural that he should, isn't it? Why, Mr. Carruthers even thanked me for reminding him of his responsibilities and said, well, that Edgar was a very lucky man to have such a caring fiancée."

"You consider yourself engaged to Edgar already, then?" Dora queried, smiling at her cousin's seriousness.

"Dora, we've been betrothed since I was fifteen," Augusta answered solemnly. "And it's not like either of us to take a vow lightly."

"To be sure," murmured Dora, biting back a giggle.

"And you'll be sure to tell Mr. Carruthers that I've confessed all my misdeeds? He was most stern with me last night. He really wants you to know all about it. Why do you suppose that is, Dora?"

Dora shrugged. She didn't know how to answer the child. Her sentiments for Carruthers were undergoing a sort of change, as he had perhaps known they would. No longer did he stand condemned, the seducer of a young and innocent girl. But this made him no more acceptable to Dora than he had been before. Good Lord, he had still asked her to become his mistress! No amount of kindness toward Edgar

Farley, nor innocence in Augusta's case, could make up for that.

Augusta was with difficulty persuaded to cut off her praises of "sweet Mr. Carruthers" and return to her bed. Dora lay awake in hers, feeling somewhat at a loss. Her anger at Carruthers, her martial insistence that he marry Augusta or face the consequences of the Brackens' wrath, had been giving Dora an outlet to the warmer passions Carruthers had stirred in her. What was she to do now about him? She finally dropped off to sleep, resolved in one thing only: she would not apologize to Carruthers for misunderstanding his relationship with Augusta. Such a dreadful man—and she still thought him dreadful—did not deserve the courtesy.

LADY BRACKEN'S REACTION to Augusta's engagement was all that her doting companion might have wished. Flanked by her grinning papa and her bashful suitor, Augusta came into the morning room much later in the morning and bluntly stated, "Mama, I'm going to be married."

Dora, who had been knotting a fringe as an accompaniment to Cousin Maud's self-satisfied monologue about Augusta's many suitors, held back her amusement.

Lady Bracken's sharp eyes flashed from her daughter, to the quaking young man so close beside her, then to her husband. "Sir Giles, this is madness," she cried. Rising from her chair, she struck her most majestic pose, hesitated a moment and crumpled to the floor.

In the ensuing scramble to get her ladyship onto a couch and restore her to consciousness, Dora took on the task of running upstairs for the smelling bottle. As soon as she got out into the hall she leaned against a wall and laughed until the tears ran down her cheeks, trying her best to muffle her hilarity.

She recovered herself eventually, and the enquiring face of the butler swam into view. "You had better deny the family to all visitors, Greaves," Dora said, and hurried up the stairs before she burst into another series of chuckles.

When Dora went back into the morning room, salts in hand, Lady Bracken had already returned to consciousness and was holding forth to her audience.

"I have never heard of such a thing, Sir Giles. Why am I to care now that this young man has a living? A living, forsooth! When some of the foremost men of property in town have been running after Augusta, you would have her throw herself away on this—this stupid boy."

Edgar Farley, very red of face, cleared his throat. "Pardon me, ma'am, but I must take exception to that characterization. I took first honours at university, after all, and I have shown the good taste to choose as my partner in life your very charming daughter."

"Oh, Edgar," sighed Augusta. She and the young man were sitting very near each other on the sofa, and she gazed up at him in open adoration.

Lady Bracken didn't dignify the young man's statement with an answer. Instead she turned on Dora. "Well, Cousin, I wouldn't have believed you had the indelicacy to intrude on what is so obviously a private family discussion."

"I expected to find you still swooning, Cousin Maud," Dora answered smoothly. She set down the smelling bottle on a table near Lady Bracken and added, "May I offer felicitations on dear Augusta's engagement?"

"Oh!" Lady Bracken's eyes blazed with anger.

"Many thanks for your kind words, Cousin, Maudie means to say," put in Sir Giles, winking at Dora. "She's a bit overcome by the good news."

"To be sure, Sir Giles. Now I'll leave you to your family conference," Dora said with a smile.

Sir Giles stood. "I'll excuse you for your own comfort, my dear, but by now I hope you realize that you are very much a member of the family." He escorted her to the door, gave her arm a friendly pat and whispered, "Go out or something, Cousin Theodora. Enjoy the day."

Dora, who had not been at all insulted by Cousin Maud's words, whatever Sir Giles might have thought, pondered his advice as she mounted the stairs again to her own room. Enjoy the day! It seemed like forever since she had planned a whole day simply around herself. She went over the possibilities in her mind: a walk to the lending library, a nap, a few hours spent reading a frivolous book. By the time she had got to her room she had decided on an amusing, if not altogether selfish, activity. She would write letters to her sisters, announcing Augusta's forthcoming marriage. The pleasure of dwelling on what Cousin Maud no doubt felt was the season's greatest tragedy would enliven an otherwise boring and repetitive chore; Dora had often wished that she might simply send off one letter to Lavinia—who was the eldest—and instruct her to send it on to the other two in turn.

Writing to Mary first, Dora had just penned the words "Our cousin Augusta has managed at last to overthrow her mother's insufferable self-satisfaction," when there was a tap on the door.

"Your pardon, ma'am, but this just come for you, and there is a footman waiting for an answer," said Betsy, depositing in front of Dora a highly scented note addressed to "Mademoiselle de Thornfield" in a flourishing, ungainly script.

Dora stared at it. "My word! Well, thank you, Betsy. It must be from—from my old French governess. Don't bother to wait. I'll go down with my answer in a moment."

"Thank you, miss, I did have the beds to do up here," said Betsy. Bobbing a little curtsey, she went out.

Dora, with shaking fingers, broke the seal: purple wax, stamped with an ornate *Y* intertwined with a cockade. After a formal greeting, the only message was a simple: "I must see you at once. Go with my footman. Y."

Go off with the footman of that creature, indeed! And into what undignified situation? Dora shook her head.

Then she thought again. By Sir Giles's authority, she had the day to enjoy herself. Yvette had already made the hysterical confession that she loved Carruthers. Was it possible that she had heard of his offer to Dora—likely from the man himself—and wanted more reassurance that she didn't have a rival in a certain quiet spinster? Or perhaps he had abused the Frenchwoman in some new way, and she wanted to warn Dora further about his horrid, violent nature.

It would be unlike a quiet spinster to go out upon such an errand of mercy. Dora twirled the quill in her fingers for quite two minutes before she rose, put the letter to Mary carefully away and folded Yvette's note into her reticule. It was with a feeling of great daring and a frisson of foreboding that she calmly walked to the wardrobe and got out her bonnet and pelisse.

CHAPTER SEVENTEEN

A YOUNG, HANDSOME and extremely muscular footman, clad in the distinctive livery Dora remembered from her other meeting with Yvette, was waiting in the lower hall of the Bracken house. Dora turned to Greaves, who stood by with a very disapproving expression on his face, and said, "Please inform the others that I'll be returning in time for dinner. This is an urgent errand." Then she nodded to the footman, and they proceeded out of the house.

The closed carriage with the cockade emblazoned on the door, which Dora also remembered, was waiting in the street. The footman ushered her into it, and the adventure, Dora supposed, was officially on. The barouche didn't travel quickly through the crowded streets, and its occupant, shrinking back carefully into the squabs to forestall being recognized in the carriage of a noted Cyprian, wondered if she misremembered the way to Charles Street. Shouldn't the coachman have turned right at the corner?

They had gone some distance in the wrong direction before Dora became suspicious. She pulled the check-string and wasn't too astonished when nothing happened.

"I am being abducted," she murmured in a kind of wonder. She had been stupid, it would seem. But it was so unlikely that anyone would abduct her that Dora really couldn't think of this experience in such a dramatic term. There was a very good chance of Yvette's greeting her at journey's end, engaging in some kind of a histrionic scene, then letting her go home. Perhaps reasons of discretion had led the Cyprian to hold this interview at a location other than Charles Street.

The carriage was bowling along ever faster in a southerly direction, to the Surrey side. Dora was astonished to glance out of the window after what seemed like a remarkably short time and see no sign of town at all, only hedgerows.

Eventually the vehicle drew to a halt. The door swung open, and the steps were let down by the same man who had escorted Dora from the house in Albemarle Street.

Dora descended, holding her back ramrod straight. "I assume you have an explanation for this extraordinary behaviour, my good man," she snapped. "I pulled the string five times."

"Very good, ma'am," responded the handsome footman, his face expressionless.

Dora looked about her. She was standing in front of a small cottage fronted by a garden which was a virtual mass of flowers and bordered by a privet hedge. It was the only house in sight. She had never seen a cottage *orné* before, though she had heard of them, and couldn't help smiling at its arched windows, miniscule turrets and ornamental thatchwork. It looked quite like an illustration for a Gothic romance.

"The mistress's country place," the footman said. "Will you walk in, ma'am?"

Dora supposed she had no choice; however, she had to try her power. "No, I'd prefer to return to London, if you please," she said. "I had no idea that we'd journey so far, and I can't be gone from home for such a long time."

"I'm afraid that will be impossible, ma'am," replied the footman, still in that smooth voice devoid of all animation. He squared his broad shoulders as he stood by Dora's side and managed to look larger than ever. The coachman, the lady passenger saw out of the corner of her eye, had also descended from his perch and was, if anything, more muscular than the other man.

Dora opened the gate in the hedge and moved down the walk. The servants didn't follow her, but she could feel them watching her every move. She knocked at the miniature castle door, and when that failed to rouse anyone, she opened it.

Within was a tiny, panelled hall which boasted as its main ornament a Tudor-era suit of armour standing near the foot of a polished wood staircase with a carved balustrade. Though she was very nervous, Dora involuntarily let out a laugh at this romantic folly. Then she turned into the room at the right, the door of which was ajar, calling out as she did so, "Miss Yvette! Are you there?"

Her voice was shaking, Dora was annoyed to note. And she had thought she was behaving with such laudable calm! The chamber, a drawing room of sorts, was empty. It was richly furnished, in the same mode as Yvette's salon in London had been, and over the little, intricately carved marble mantelpiece hung a portrait of Yvette, unclothed, much like the one at which Dora had blushed in Charles Street.

Somehow it was comforting to see these familiar signs of Yvette's occupancy; Dora at least knew that she hadn't been tricked by someone else. Sitting down rather gingerly on a red velvet sofa in the middle of the room, she prepared to wait. A novel was lying open on its spine on an adjacent marble-topped table, and Dora picked it up. She was soon endeavouring to remember her irregular verbs, for she hadn't had occasion to use more than the rare, tonnish French phrase since the seminary.

Time passed, and Dora removed her pelisse and bonnet and made up the fire, all the while struggling with the novel.

So absorbed did she become in her task—for the page she had hit upon, a letter from a certain Vicomte de Valmont to a Marquise de Merteuil, looked to be well worth translating—that she didn't notice the door open.

"Eh, what?" boomed a rusty voice. "A charming bit you are indeed. Haven't we met, my pretty?"

Dora's head jerked up, and she found herself looking into the rheumy eyes of General Sir Percival Laughton!

Snapping the book shut, she rose to her feet. "Why, General," she said loudly, remembering his infirmity, "what a surprise. Are you visiting Mademoiselle Yvette, too?"

The general, leering awfully, cocked an ear. "What's that? Yvette? The minx said I'd find it worth me while to visit here, and so it proves, m'dear. Met her at the Cyprians' ball yesternight, y'know, and asked if she knew of any new mutton, and demmed if she didn't promise me a rare treat."

Dora rolled her eyes, and the day took a definite turn for the worse. So the gentlemen had gone on to the Cyprians' ball after Lady Bracken's decorous dinner the night before! How typical. She'd wager Mr. Carruthers had made one of the party, as well. But her wrath now was directed at Yvette. "That—that awful woman. How could she? Is she going to be here?" she got out, stepping carefully across the room away from her elderly companion.

The general heard not a word of this. He did see the indignant face of his "bit," though, and this prompted him to chuckle in delight as he lumbered unsteadily across the room—his gout had been paining him lately—and snatched at her sleeve. Dora swatted at his gloved hand with her reticule, wishing she hadn't dropped the book.

Her attacker, undeterred, muttered something about liking a woman with spirit. "Been at this trade long, dearie?" he added with a wink. "It's worth another five guineas if you'd—"

"Sir!" Dora shouted. "I'm not a doxy!"

Sir Percival paused in his latest effort to grasp his prey' waist and considered this statement, which he had defi nitely heard. The servants outside had probably heard it too, Dora thought with pride in her lung power. Finally h responded, "Nonsense, my lovely. You're in this house ain't you? Now come over here and sit on my knee."

Dora had been desperately looking about the room fo something she might use to break over the general's head Finally her eyes lit upon a crystal decanter, full of a rub liquid, and another, more subtle idea came to her.

"General," she said, trying to speak loudly and at th same time in a caressing, acquiescent voice, "do let's hav a drink together... first." She dimpled and batted her eyes feeling inexpressibly foolish as she did so.

The old man beamed at this sensible suggestion, sittin down on one end of the sofa. Dora tripped across the roon in the manner of an operatic chambermaid, poured two glasses of the stuff—whatever it was—and delivered on into the hand of her admirer. She took a chair across from him, trying to ignore the fact that he was patting his lap i a suggestive manner, and sipped from her own glass.

"Another? Certainly, sir," she chirped out five second later, when the general had drained his goblet.

"Washy stuff," grumbled Sir Percival, but he suffered Dora to pour him another of the same, which disappeared as quickly.

By his third glass Dora was beginning to despair of get ting this old reprobate insensibly drunk on a liquor he de scribed as washy, and was considering whether it might no be more effective to bash him over the head with the decan ter. Luckily the ceremony of drinking was too serious a thing to the general to allow for grasping at his ladybird at th same time. As long as the wine held out, he would drink it and would offer no more threat to Dora than the occasional invitation to sit upon his knee like a good girl, which she, with blushes and false giggling, declined.

With a sinking heart, Dora poured out the last of the ruby wine into Sir Percival's glass.

"Pretty wench," snorted the general. "We'll be moving along upstairs, what?" He drained the glass.

"Oh, splendid, sir," shouted Dora. "Do let me go up first and make ready for you."

The general nodded affably, lurched to his feet and snaffled Dora's glass of wine, which she had hardly touched, from the table across from the sofa.

Dora closed the drawing-room door behind her and stood for the merest second, leaning against it and considering her options. She was confident that, one way or another, she could hold off the general forever, if need be; but how tedious that sounded! There were four directions she might go: the parlour opposite; out through the front, the way she had entered; into what must be the servants' quarters through a door under the stairs; or—last choice—up those stairs. Dora tried the front door first, not too shocked to find it was locked up tight, probably barred from the outside. The other parlour door wouldn't open, either, thus quashing any hopes she might have had of exiting through French doors or a window. And a cursory inspection of the back door proved it, too, was barricaded against any escape attempt. Yvette, or her minions, had been thorough.

It had by now occurred to Dora that the fair owner of this house, despite her assurance to the contrary, was still consumed with jealousy of her spinster rival. But why Yvette should set General Laughton on Dora in such a carefully contrived way was a mystery. The Cyprian must realize that anyone under fifty with the requisite number of wits was

well able to outmanoeuvre the general. And what good
would it be, in any case, to engineer Miss Thornfield's ruin?

Dora stood wavering in the hall next to the suit of armour. To go upstairs seemed foolish, but at least it would
put distance between her and Sir Percival. She ran up, noticing even in her distress the fine quality of the Oriental
carpet beneath her feet; such prosperity was a questionable
lesson on the wages of sin.

There were several bedrooms on the upper floor, none of
which were locked and none of which seemed more sinister
than another. Dora finally chose a sitting room, reasoning
that it was better not to go near a bed at this juncture, and
tried to get her bearings. The window of this fluffy, pink-
decorated chamber—didn't Yvette know any other colours?—gave on the front of the house, and Dora could see
that, though the coach had disappeared, the footman and
the coachman were still at the front gate, talking and looking as large and competent as ever. She sighed and walked
into the bedroom across the hall.

Pushing back rose-velvet draperies from the window in
that chamber, she gazed on a small back garden with a very
high wall. There didn't seem to be a gate, but over the wall
there was a beech wood. Dora frowned. If one could manage to climb that wall and get into the wood... But there
remained the problem of getting down from this ornamental turret window. It was a sheer drop to the ground, unre-
lieved by even a patch of ivy or a bush that might break a
person's fall.

Muttering terrible things about Yvette and wishing she
had stayed home to write letters, Dora went out into the hall
to investigate another bedroom.

"There you are, me beauty," cried the general, throwing
stout arms about her waist.

Dora was more exasperated than frightened by now. "General, I *order* you to stop this," she exclaimed, trying to wriggle out of his unexpectedly tight grip.

"Fightin' woman, can't ask for more," grunted the general. One of his beefy hands landed on Dora's hitherto untouched backside. "Demmed if this ain't more fun than I thought it'd be. Now we have met before, ain't we, dear? Last night at the Argyle Rooms, wasn't it?"

"I shall scream," uttered Dora in a tone which was already very near to her threat.

Chuckling, the general backed his prize into one of the bedrooms. Dora, fighting every step of the way, suddenly fell backward and had the breath knocked out of her. She was on the bed, and General Laughton was on top of her.

"Help!" she shrieked into the tangle of bed curtains, pillows, arms and legs. With one hand she resolutely pushed the general's leering face to one side, forestalling his attempt to snatch a kiss.

"Well, Miss Thornfield," came an amused voice from the doorway. "What have we here?"

CHAPTER EIGHTEEN

SOMEWHAT EARLIER that same day, Lawrence Carruthers, anticipating a good laugh, had called in at the Bracken house in Albemarle Street. He knew that Augusta Bracken was engaged to tell Miss Thornfield "everything" about her intrigue with himself; and he also knew that Edgar Farley was planning to make formal application for the young lady's hand. Dora's recognition of her mistake, added to Lady Bracken's discomfiture at the betrothal, were spectacles too good to pass up. Or so thought the irreverent Mr. Carruthers.

"The family is not at home," intoned Greaves, bowing regretfully as he took Carruthers's card.

"Pity. None of them? Miss Thornfield, perhaps?"

The butler sniffed. "Gone out, sir, and the rest of the household is indisposed."

"Out, you say?" Carruthers smiled genially, expecting Greaves to confide the lady's errand. He would catch up with her in shop or park and have it out at last. Augusta Bracken, if she was true to her word at all, would have made the long-overdue confession to her cousin by now, and Carruthers had no desire to delay the unprecedented pleasure of listening to Dora admit she'd been wrong about him.

Greaves looked very disapproving indeed. Then he shot an appraising glance at the gentleman, seeming to like what he saw. "You're a good friend to the family, sir, and I say it don't do for a young lady—well, even not so young a lady—

to go jauntering off alone in a closed carriage. Our Betsy—the chambermaid, sir—mentioned that Miss Thornfield had received a note from her old French governess, but it does seem a bit irregular, sir, that she would go off without a word to the rest of the household. I was to tell her ladyship that Miss Thornfield will be back for dinner.''

"Her French governess, you say?" Carruthers's lips curved upward into a wicked smile. "Was this equipage a very shiny barouche, trimmed in red, and did the servants dress in red and purple livery?"

"Why, yes, sir."

Carruthers grinned. "That lady, the old governess, is known to me. Never you fear, Greaves, I'll go along to her house and fetch Miss Thornfield back in time for dinner."

"It lacks only an hour to that time, sir. We are dining early due to a theatre party this evening." Greaves bowed, and his habitually stern expression relaxed a bit as Mr. Carruthers turned and ran down the stairs.

Another stiff and proper butler was soon opening a door to Mr. Carruthers. "How d'ye do, Farnham. Is your mistress at home? I expect she has a guest, but you may announce me."

Farnham inclined his head. "Guest? No, Mademoiselle is alone, sir, but I will have to ascertain whether she is receiving at present."

Carruthers laughed at this, headed toward the rose salon, and said over his shoulder, "Tell her I'm in here and she'd better be quick." He was leaning against the ornate mantelpiece, wondering if Yvette had been subjecting Dora to some new lies, when the door burst open and the Cyprian sailed in.

"Laurent!" she exclaimed, rushing across the room. White draperies swirled round her, and Carruthers couldn't help noticing that the garment was transparent. "Ah, how pleased I am to see you, *chéri*."

"Where, Yvette, is Miss Thornfield?" Carruthers enquired, holding the woman off with one arm.

Yvette halted in pretty confusion. "A thorn? What is this, my dearest?"

"Yvette, don't be coy. I happen to know that your carriage picked up Miss Theodora Thornfield in Albemarle Street earlier today. Good God, did you dispose of her already?" Carruthers still assumed that Dora was on the premises—perhaps Yvette had sought to shock a proper spinster further by receiving her in the boudoir—but his smile had changed, in the wink of an eye, into a threatening frown.

Yvette shrugged, which action took her diaphanous garment even further down her arms and exposed nearly all of her bosom to the interested observer. "Laurent, there is no one here with me. You may search the premises if you like."

"Then where is she, my sly darling?" Carruthers favoured Yvette with his most penetrating and suspicious gaze. She dropped her eyes under his scrutiny.

"I know not what you are talking about," she mumbled in the thick French accent she reserved for difficult times.

"Yvette, I'm warning you."

Yvette had been looking down at the floor, but suddenly she raised her eyes. "Well, if you must know, *chéri*, your little friend begged to borrow my coach. I wrote to tell her she might go where she liked. It is doubtless that she has another lover somewhere, and needs to be discreet. After all, the creature still maintains the fiction of innocent *vieille fille*." Another expressive, and revealing, shrug.

"You're lying through your teeth," snapped Carruthers, grasping his ex-mistress by her unclothed shoulders. "What in the name of heaven possessed you to meddle in the life of a respectable woman, and where have you had her spirited off to? And for what daft reason?''

''The lady's affairs are her own,'' Yvette said in a fine imitation of feminine loyalty. ''That she chooses you to believe her an *innocente* is also her business. Ah, she won't fool you for long. A man of the world—'' and she let her warm dark eyes linger admiringly on Carruthers's face ''—would never be taken in by the pose of untried virgin, even from one so cunning.''

''My dear, if I don't slap your face and throttle you into insensibility for those ill-judged words, it is only because I pity you more than I blame you for bandying about the name of that lady,'' said Carruthers in a quiet, tense voice. ''Will you tell me where she is?''

Yvette hesitated. Her eyes stared up into Laurent's and found only cold indifference tempered by anger. ''She mentioned using my little house.''

''The Surrey cottage? Now is this the truth, Yvette? Is she there?'' Carruthers's voice was full of such concern that Yvette had difficulty in holding her fingernails sheathed, longing as she was to rake them across his face for displaying such emotion toward another woman.

''She is there,'' she spat, wrenching herself from the man's grip. She folded her arms under her bosom, accentuating its fullness even more, and turned away from him. He was a madman! To refuse this—the loveliest negligée in London, covering the most luscious body—for the awkward embraces of a respectable spinster! Well, if he sought his blameless Miss Thornfield out now, he would have quite the surprise.

Carruthers, without another word, was heading for the door and, Yvette suspected, out of her life. ''She will not thank you for interfering in her *métier*,'' she cried.

He looked back. His smile was ironic, amused. "My poor creature, you've given it your best, but do know when to quit. I've reason to believe that you have had Miss Thornfield to your house, on purpose to shock her, and that you gave her to think that I planned her to be my next mistress. Won't that suffice for your interference in the young woman's life?"

"Monstre!" shrieked Yvette.

Carruthers sighed. "If I don't see that you pay for this, my dear, it's only because I have the feeling that you're already paying, and paying dearly, every day. Goodbye."

Yvette let out an angry gasp. By the time a plaster statuette crashed against the door, Carruthers had already slammed it shut.

IN THE BRACKEN HOUSE, meanwhile, an armed truce of sorts had been declared. Sir Giles, with a wickedly pleased expression in his eyes which his lady found heartless, had retired to his library, where he was drawing up a draft of the marriage settlements which could be gone over later with Carruthers, in his capacity as Edgar Farley's adviser. Lady Bracken found the strength to drag herself upstairs where, she told the others in long-suffering tones, she planned to remain prostrate until the dreadful news had sunk in. This left Augusta and Edgar tête-à-tête in the morning room, and they made good use of the unexpected treat to get to know each other better. How much better, was circumscribed only by the fact that Greaves, before ten minutes had passed, took care to open the door and leave it ajar, clearing his throat loudly as he did so.

"Oh, Edgar," sighed Augusta, detaching herself gently from her young man's arms when this occurred, "to think that we'll be married, after all."

"Not if your mother has her way," Edgar reminded her, planting a fairly chaste kiss on her cheek as he glanced through the doorway at the hovering Greaves.

"Oh, but Papa is with us, and that's all that matters. Only Mama will make it so uncomfortable. What do you think of marrying very soon, my love, to get me out of the house?" Augusta glanced up brightly. "Poor Dora, though. With Mama in such a foul mood she'll lead a dog's life."

"Your cousin Miss Thornfield, you mean?" enquired Edgar.

"Yes, stuck as she is being Mama's companion, she'll be left to hard times when I escape. Not that that will stop me, mind you." And Augusta gave her young clergyman her most ardent gaze.

Edgar responded in the best way possible, by kissing her again—and not on the cheek!

Greaves was called from the observation of these improprieties by a knock at the door. He opened it to Captain Thomas Laughton.

"The family is not at home, sir," the butler recited.

"Oh, what a pity. I have here a letter for Lady Bracken that is supposed to be most urgent," responded the captain, holding out a note with a purple seal.

"A letter?" Greaves paused. Urgency was usually to be heeded, so seldom it occurred. And the captain's face was grim. Also, this missive looked exactly like the one Miss Thornfield had received earlier in the day. "I will take it to her ladyship. She is indisposed, but may want to rouse herself for its perusal. You are certain of its urgency, sir?"

"More or less. The whole situation is quite the mystery to me," Laughton answered more cheerfully. He entered to wait in the hall.

The butler summoned a footman, who in turn transported the letter to Lady Bracken's dresser, who, Greaves assured the captain, would take it in to Madam without delay.

"I'm required to wait for an answer," said the captain, leaning back at his ease in one of the hard chairs in the hall. He peeked into the morning room, noticed a young couple cuddling on the sofa and, in a comradely spirit, reached out and pushed the door shut.

Before five minutes had passed, Meeker came running down the stairs. "Oh, Captain, sir," she cried, "I'm to say her ladyship will be with you in a moment."

Laughton nodded and stood up in anticipation of this treat.

When the lady swept down the stairs, she was dressed in outdoor things and had a hard, martial gleam in her eye. She carried the letter.

"Have you read this, Captain?" she asked, when hurried greetings had been exchanged.

"No, but it was enclosed in one to me, and if it was similar, I'd say we should be off. I take it you are planning to come along? Your presence is required so that we may enter, as I understand it."

"Yes, indeed. Greaves," said Lady Bracken, "tell Sir Giles—and Miss Augusta, to be sure—that I will return as soon as I can. Perhaps we ought to give up the theatre for this evening."

"And does your ladyship return to dine?"

Lady Bracken considered this carefully. "Keep it back one hour. If I've not returned beforehand, Sir Giles will have to eat with Miss Augusta and that horrid boy."

"Very good, madam. And Miss Thornfield?"

"Her!" Lady Bracken sniffed in her most haughty manner. "That trollop will not be coming back here at all, if I have anything to say about it. And I most certainly do."

The butler bowed, not knowing what answer to make to this extraordinary statement.

Captain Laughton was looking at Lady Bracken in a decidedly unfriendly way as he escorted her outside to the vehicle he had waiting. The anonymous letter he had received, in which Lady Bracken's had been enclosed, had made him understand that he and the lady were riding to Miss Thornfield's rescue. She was in some undisclosed danger out in the country, and Lady Bracken's presence was necessary if the abductors—whoever they were—were to be induced to free Dora.

Lady Bracken lost no time in disabusing Captain Laughton of the notion that Miss Thornfield was anyone's victim. *Her* letter had made the sordid situation quite clear.

CHAPTER NINETEEN

DORA STRUGGLED AND PANTED. Although there was someone else in the room now, it seemed no interruption could
stop General Sir Percival when he was so near to the pleasures of dalliance. "Help," she tried to cry again, and when
she only uttered a sort of squeak, she realized her admirer
was crushing her chest. Finally she felt the old gentleman's
frame being hauled off her own.

"Pardon my uncle's exuberance, Miss Thornfield," said
Captain Laughton with a grin. "Now, Uncle." And he
dragged the older man across the room to a chair.

"Demmed interference," snorted the general, fighting his
nephew every step of the way. "A prime bit, I tell you.
P'raps she'll do you tomorrow night."

"Uncle, if this lady forgives you for your shocking lapse,
you may consider yourself a lucky man. And since I can't
call out my own elderly relation, you may consider yourself
a live one."

"Eh?" croaked the general.

Dora, smiling weakly, sat up on the dishevelled bed and
gasped in horror. Standing in the doorway of the bedroom
was Lady Bracken!

"Cousin!" said that lady, glaring and holding her hand
to her heart. "I had no notion your depravity had sunk to
such loathsome depths. To think that I've opened my lovely
home, exposed my innocent daughter to a—a courtesan!"
She stalked into the room and wagged a finger in Dora's in-

credulous face. "All those times you said you were walking, or visiting Lady Lavenham's, I'll wager you were pursuing your vile trade. Saving for your old age, is it? Or are you merely one of those disgusting creatures who live only to satisfy their animal lust?"

Dora sighed and put her hand to her head. She might burst out laughing or crying in the next moments, and she wasn't sure she cared which.

"And there will be no covering this up, you disgraceful strumpet," continued Lady Bracken, her voice shrill. "I'll write to all your sisters by the next post, and I doubt you'll find their homes open to you when I've finished informing them of this sickening situation. I won't be quiet, you may depend upon it, for revealing your disgusting sham to society is far more important to me than preserving the family dignity—which is as it should be, for any family willing to cover up for such revolting goings-on would not be worth its salt. As for my home, that you must never pollute again with your meek, innocent airs and your dark perversions."

During this tirade, Captain Laughton had succeeded in removing his half-bosky uncle from the room and depositing him in the sitting room across the way. He now strode back into the bedroom, approached the ladies and, to Lady Bracken's obvious horror, took a seat beside Dora on the bed.

"Miss Thornfield," he began carefully, taking her by the hand, "I believe you must have an enemy. Do you know anyone who would want to see you ruined?"

Dora hesitated. She knew already that Yvette had engineered this near-disaster with the general, and assumed that the Cyprian had seen to it that Laughton and Lady Bracken had been drawn to the scene, perhaps in the hope they would come upon Dora in a more intimate position than the one they'd saved her from. But she could hardly admit to being acquainted with the creature; that would do her reputation as much harm as Yvette had tried to do already. Besides, there was that question of the sworn promise to the courtesan, never to reveal their meeting. Dora had made a solemn vow.

"I don't know of any enemies," she said.

"Enemies! Really, Captain," snapped Lady Bracken, who had retreated to a place near the door. "We have found out what some kind soul meant for us to find out, and that is that. Gracious, you men are sometimes too trusting for your own good. Heaven only knows how you're able to conduct any business of importance."

Dora turned her eyes to Captain Laughton. "A kind soul?"

The captain sighed. "I received an anonymous letter today, telling me you were in an unspecified danger at this location in Surrey. Enclosed was a letter to her ladyship, which proved to be a bit less vague in its contents."

"You mean it said the truth," put in Lady Bracken. She fished in her reticule and came up with a piece of paper, then strode back to the bed and rattled it at Dora. "I must be grateful to this informant, whoever it may be, for opening my eyes to your true colours, Cousin. Oh! I hate to admit you own that title. To think that our family has been a breeding ground for such . . . such . . ."

Words failed the lady, and dropping the letter, she moved to a chair far away from the two on the bed.

Dora snatched the paper and read, in Yvette's distinctive handwriting:

Madame will be interested to know that she has harboured in her bosom a *vipère*. The Thornfield has rendezvous with one of her well-paying lovers this afternoon, at a place the bearer of this letter can take you to.

"Good Lord," said Dora, "I suppose they sent you along, Captain, so that you'd be able to deal with the general."

"I must assume that was the idea," said the captain with a shrug. "I ought to mention, my letter indicated that I wouldn't gain entrance to your prison unless I brought Lady Bracken. I see now that the person was trying to ensure your ruin. Whoever it was ought to have known that I would not believe such things of you, but they were apparently certain that Lady Bracken would." He paused and looked into Dora's eyes. "Well? Can you tell us how you were brought here? Were you... Did they drug you?"

Dora had to dissimulate again. "Well, I was told that a certain friend of mine had to see me at once on a matter of great importance. There was a carriage ready to convey me to what I thought was another street in London. By the time I realized that we were heading out of town, I couldn't do anything. And when I arrived here, the coachman and his man forced me to enter this house."

"Ah. I suppose they would be the two very large characters in furze breeches and torn coats who were guarding the door?"

Well! Yvette had apparently had her men change out of their livery. The woman was clever, all right. "They must be the same ones," Dora said. "The men were very large."

"They turned tail and disappeared as soon as they let us in," the captain informed her. "What I don't understand is how my uncle could be a party to this. Well," he added, "let me qualify that statement. Uncle Percival has never been trustworthy in his cups, nor has he ever been known to turn down, er, feminine companionship."

"Someone told him a woman of the town was awaiting him here," Dora muttered in the direction of the carpet. Her face reddened awfully.

"And so you were!" cried Lady Bracken. "I suppose I should pity you, shameless creature, but such a new evidence of deception is beyond anything. If you were enticed here, it was only by the lure of gold, or of sin."

Dora sighed and leaned her head on her hands.

"Oh, stow it, Lady Bracken," the gallant captain said in Dora's defence. Not even pausing to acknowledge her ladyship's splutterings of ill-use, he patted Dora's shoulder. "I ought to take you home," he suggested. "You're overwrought, my dear. My blasted uncle, and your unknown enemy, have conspired to put you through what no young woman should face."

"Oh, don't blame Sir Percival," said Dora. "He only thought what he was led to believe, and what with his unfortunate tendency to deafness, he didn't pay attention to my explanations."

"No doubt he was chosen as your seducer for that very reason," the captain said. "Well, Uncle ought to have known reluctance when he saw it."

"Exactly what I say," chimed in Lady Bracken. "Reluctance, my foot. We come upon them, writhing about in bed, and you dare to believe this trollop when she says she was drawn here by a ruse? Captain, I can stand no more. I am leaving now in your carriage, and if you care to accompany me you had better hurry. Leave the creature to wallow in her own muck. I've had too many shocks for one day." And her ladyship rose majestically, drifted across the room with deliberate languor and paused in the doorway. "Well, Captain?"

"I must take Miss Thornfield home, and I'll thank you not to appropriate my vehicle, my lady," responded

Laughton, his breast seeming to swell with gallantry. Dora
looked at him with a grateful smile.

"Home! And where does she intend to go? She may never
darken my door again naturally, and if you think to take her
to your own rooms you can be sure all of London will know
of that by morning," Lady Bracken promised. Then she
turned on her heel for the requisite majestic exit and nearly
ran up against the solid form of Mr. Lawrence Carruthers.

"I believe, my lady, that the question of Miss
Thornfield's home is best answered by me," said that
gentleman, stepping past Lady Bracken into the room.

Dora, after one stunned look into his face, hung her head.
The day had lacked only this. For the first time she became
aware of her disarranged garments and tumbled hair, and
she could feel Carruthers's eyes, a blend of anxiety and ardent affection, running over her.

"Oh, Dora!" cried a feminine voice, and Lady Lavenham
ran into the room and took a seat on the bed at Dora's other
side.

"Amelia?" Dora had never been so glad to see anyone in
her life. She noted that her friend was wearing a dark veil,
suitable to a clandestine appointment, and this made her
smile.

"Carruthers brought me along to play propriety," Amelia
explained. "How do you do, Captain, Lady Bracken. We
didn't know someone would beat us to the rescue."

"Rescue!" sniffed Lady Bracken. "Your friend from
school, Lady Lavenham, and my cousin, has been hiding a
career as a lightskirt behind her façade of meek spinster.
And I, for one, consider it my duty to publish her shame to
society. If I were you I'd do the same."

Amelia burst out laughing.

Laughton had risen and shaken hands with Carruthers, and the two men now proceeded to compare notes, their voices lowered.

"Do let us hear you, Captain," said Lady Bracken.

Not Captain Laughton, but Carruthers, looked up and inclined his head. "We were merely saying that your cousin has been victimized by some low creature who has a reason to wish her harm. General Laughton, forsooth! Only the greatest beast in nature would foist that old reprobate on this lady. And I, for one, can think of only one person who would be cruel enough to do this dreadful thing." He glared at Lady Bracken.

Amelia saw at once where Carruthers was leading. "Maud! For shame!" she cried. "Now I know you've been jealous of your cousin's success with the men, which has certainly been to your daughter's detriment, but to do this! What will Lady Cowper say? Or Madame de Lieven?"

Dora judged it best to remain silent at this point, conceding that, though the accusation was false, Cousin Maud might have played a conscious part in this scheme had she known about it.

"What? What?" Lady Bracken, holding her hand at her heart again, came all the way back into the room and plopped into the nearest chair, a gilded one covered in red velvet. "Good Lord! The absolute gall! As if I would plot something like this to discredit that woman. From what I've seen, she needs none of my help, for she is already on the road to ruin." Her cold dark eyes surveyed Dora menacingly. "Don't think I'll keep quiet about this to Sir James Perry, either. To think of you, living in the same house as his sweet, innocent daughters. It doesn't bear thinking of!" She shook her head in sadness. "Many loose women have tried to establish themselves by marriage, I'd wager, but that's one deception you won't pull off, Cousin."

"Oh, Cousin Maud," Dora sighed. "Why don't you go away? I've done nothing wrong, and I'm tired of listening to you call me names."

"I believe the lady is right, madam," said Carruthers. "This is none of her fault, I can swear to that, and she's been subjected to more than enough of your abuse." He turned to Laughton. "Captain, may I prevail upon you to take her ladyship home? And do remind her that no one in the ton will take kindly to her having perpetrated this little scheme. It's quite unworthy of Sir Giles's wife, in fact. You might remind her of how fond her husband and her daughter both are of Miss Thornfield, and of how unforgiving society can be regarding this sort of game."

"And remind her further that I am on intimate terms with most of the ton's sharpest tongues," Amelia put in gaily from her place by Dora's side.

The captain nodded, only his twinkling blue eyes betraying his enjoyment as Lady Bracken huffed and gasped at each new threat. He and Carruthers shook hands again. Then Laughton went back to the bed and knelt before Dora.

"My dear, I would have thought myself the proper person to rescue you from this, but I was looking at your face just now when a certain other person entered the room. I'm not the one, am I?"

"Oh, Captain," sighed Dora in true distress, reaching out to touch his face. The pleasant, ruddy features were serious and sad.

"How gallant," Amelia burst out. "Oh, dear, I do feel de trop. Shall we all leave you alone?"

"No, my lady—" Captain Laughton rose to his feet and kissed Dora's hand "—we've just established that you shouldn't. Good afternoon." He retraced his steps to the door, where Lady Bracken was standing not far from Carruthers. Both of them had been observing the scene,

Carruthers with a startled face that betrayed his jealousy, her ladyship with blatant disgust. "Come, ma'am," said the captain. "You might yet make it home in time for dinner."

"Well!" The tender words Lady Bracken had just witnessed had unleashed all her fury. "Captain, I was going to break it to you gently, but you might as well know now that my daughter, Augusta, has become betrothed to another man. And at this moment I'm glad of it, you—you bounder!"

"Ah, I can see it will be a pleasant ride home," replied the captain to the room at large. "I might be forced to ride on the box. But what of my uncle?"

The group thought the subject over for a moment. General Laughton's snores had been audible for some time from the room across the hall. "Why not leave him here to sleep it off?" Carruthers suggested. "Whoever owns this house might not be pleased to find him here, but that needn't be our concern."

"Famous idea, Carruthers," said the captain with a hearty laugh. "Good night, then, and, Miss Thornfield, I am your most obedient."

He grasped Lady Bracken by the arm and escorted her away. She left the room with not a backward glance.

When they had gone, Amelia looked round her with interest. "So this is a house of shame. How very intriguing." She rose from the bed to examine more closely the various ornaments and the superfluity of mirrors. "Your Yvette has shocking taste, Carruthers."

"Amelia!" gasped Dora. "You know?"

Carruthers had approached Dora and was looking at her quizzically. He now said, "She is no longer *my* Yvette, Lady Lavenham."

"You did intend to replace her, did you not? With me," Dora said. "You can't have forgotten what I told you,

Amelia. This man, who calls himself a gentleman, offered a *carte blanche* to me the other day, and nothing will stop him from insisting that I accept it.''

"Oh, Dora," Amelia said with a chuckle. Seeing her friend's indignant expression, she added, "Do pardon me, my dear, but this is so very amusing. Carruthers to be offering *carte blanche* to a sister of Sir Leonard Fitzhugh and Lord MacDonald, not to mention Mr. What's-his-name, Lavinia's husband.''

Dora looked up sharply. She had never thought of it that way. "I consider myself to be alone in the world," she protested.

Tossing her bright head, Amelia said, "Oh, come now, my dear. I know you're penniless and proud and all that, but you do have connections. You are my intimate friend, after all, and many a more foolish man than Carruthers—your pardon, sir—would think twice before offending me.''

"Well, then," said Dora, "Mr. Carruthers is quite bold, to risk your enmity.''

Carruthers cast an appealing look at Amelia, who understood at once and said, "Oh, I must be going downstairs. This Yvette has such an interesting house that I don't want to miss a single thing.''

"Amelia!" groaned Dora.

"No, don't thank me, my love, and rest assured that my lips are sealed. No one will ever hear it from me that you've been alone with a gentleman in the bedroom of the most exclusive high-flyer in town." Amelia burst out in giggles at the end of her speech and fled out the door, looking very mischievous.

"Amelia!" Dora called out, standing up to run after her perfidious friend. She noticed for the first time that there was a massive rent in the front of her skirt, no doubt a souvenir of General Laughton's ardour.

"Good Lord, my dear," Carruthers said, stepping for ward and effectively cutting off the lady's avenue of es cape, "you'd do much better to stay. You aren't in any fi condition to be going anywhere."

Dora let out a furious little sound of distress and clenched her fists.

And Carruthers took another step, captured her in hi arms, and began to kiss her and kiss her, giving her n chance to do anything but respond with all the longing in her heart.

CHAPTER TWENTY

DORA FELT HERSELF FLOATING in a world of new sensation. Everything that had ever happened to her was forgotten. Thought was of no importance; the chief thing was to keep kissing, to run her hands over the slightly rough cheek so near her own, to mould tighter to the hard-muscled body that held her fast.

"Ah," sighed Carruthers, pausing for breath. "Marry me soon, love. I can't stand too much more of this."

Dora blinked, and the world righted itself. "Marry you?" she whispered, searching his face.

"You've had two days to consider my proposal. I know you wouldn't want to rush into a decision," the gentleman said, with a crooked smile.

"Please. Wait a minute." Dora stepped back in his arms, for he wouldn't let her go completely. "The other day, at your country house, you asked me to be your mistress and nothing else."

"Did I?" His voice was teasing, and his lips descended on hers again.

She pulled away, for this was no problem that could be solved by a touch. "Do you deny it? You didn't when I accused you so."

"Well, I was so astonished that you could think such a thing, especially when coupled with the belief that I had seduced your cousin Augusta." Carruthers's lips twitched.

"Seduce that chit! How could you believe me capable of that? I ought to be angry with you, my dear."

Dora blushed and looked away. "I chanced to overhear you talking. I know it was inexcusable for me to eavesdrop, but your words gave every indication that the worst had occurred. However—" she looked up bravely into his eyes "—I do admit I was wrong. She told me the whole story this morning. And I have to say, sir, that you've been wonderfully generous to the young people."

Carruthers accepted the compliment with a shrug and a chuckle. His fingers caressed Dora's neck, doing terrible things to her concentration. "Your cousin didn't give me much chance to be otherwise, and the living happened to have fallen vacant. Those children will be happy, even if the young lady's mother won't. Now say you'll marry me and we'll get back to—" his lips brushed her forehead, a slow caress that stirred up as much longing as any of his more passionate salutes had done "—more pleasurable activities."

"No." Dora looked at him resolutely. "It won't do, I tell you. The other day you didn't say a word of love or marriage. It was all . . . things a man would say to his mistress." He had said he wanted her, and ordered her to admit she wanted him. That was all Dora could remember, aside from the physical contact. Her eyes were suddenly woeful as they searched his. "Amelia's talk of my connections and the world's opinion might have led you to change a proposition to a proposal, but I know. I've known all along what you meant to make of me."

"My dear," said Carruthers, "if I omitted to mention marriage the other day, it's only because you cut our interview short. But I understand that you'd been prejudiced against me. Oh, and I don't blame you a bit for believing

Yvette when she put on such a very good act for your benefit.''

"What?" Dora's eyes widened. "There's no possible way you could know anything about— That is, what do you mean?''

"I mean that my former mistress had you to her house and regaled you with a tale of how I was setting you up as her successor. You, my dear love, are not the only one with the habit of listening at doors, but I would judge that, unlike Yvette's butler, you can't be bought with a handful of gold.''

"She made me swear on my mother's grave that I'd never tell about my visit," Dora murmured into his coat-front. "Poor creature! She is so very much in love with you.''

"I doubt that," returned Carruthers. "I will concede that I'm somewhat of a catch, and I suspect she's been angling for marriage. But she failed in her attempt, and I'm done keeping mistresses. Unless you would choose to take on the position?" He raised an ironic eyebrow.

Dora's visage had darkened awfully before she realized that he was joking. "You revolting man! Which is it to be, wife or mistress?''

"Why, both, of course," stated Mr. Carruthers. "I admit that in many ways mistress would be the preferable role. As it is, my poor love, you'll have to trip down the aisle of some London church in full view of the ton, attended perhaps by cousin Augusta and the Perry sisters. Not a very pleasant prospect.''

"We could always elope," said Dora, shuddering at this picture.

"Ah, but this isn't a runaway match, is it now? Do I dare think your sisters will approve me?''

"Are you a man?" Dora queried with a cynical shrug of her shoulders. "Well, never mind them. What was it that you said about getting back to a more pleasurable activity?"

Carruthers's arms tightened about Dora's waist as her own closed around his neck. Their lips met for the first time in perfect understanding. "I do love you, you know," whispered Dora.

"I adore you, my lovely bride," murmured Carruthers.

"Eh, what?" rasped a voice from the doorway, and the couple turned to see General Sir Percival Laughton standing, rumpled and disgruntled, in the hall. "That you, young Carruthers? You'll have her tomorrow, lad. Prime bit. Spirit. Like that in a woman."

Without ceremony, Carruthers crossed and slammed the door in the gentleman's face.

"Perhaps not tomorrow," he whispered a moment later, running his fingers through Dora's curls, "but I'll have you, my sweet and modest spinster. I'll have you."

His lady responded with a mischievous smile, and she stood on tiptoe to murmur into his ear, "I see no reason why you should not, *Laurent*."

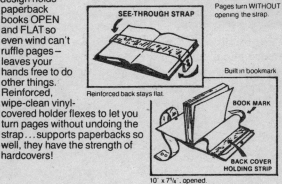